Cities on Fire:

A Family's Apocalypse

Apocalypse: A Family's Survival Story

by

AJ Newman

*

This book is dedicated to Patsy, my beautiful wife of over thirty years who assists with everything from Beta reading to censor duties. She enables me to write, golf, and enjoy my life with her and our mob of Shih Tzus.

Thanks to Cliff Deane for beta reading and being a great friend who I can bounce ideas off.

This book is a work of fiction. All events, names characters, and places are the product of the author's imagination or are used as a fictitious event. That means that I thought up this whole book from my imagination and nothing in it is true.

*

Books by AJ Newman

A Family's Apocalypse series:
Cities on Fire   Family Survival (late summer 2017)

After the Solar Flare - a Post-Apocalyptic series:
Alone in the Apocalypse   Adventures in the Apocalypse*

After the EMP series:
The Day America Died New Beginnings
The Day America Died Old Enemies
The Day America Died Frozen Apocalypse

"The Adventures of John Harris" - a Post-Apocalyptic America series:
Surviving   Hell in the Homeland   Tyranny in the Homeland
Revenge in the Homeland...Apocalypse in the Homeland   John Returns

"A Samantha Jones Murder Mystery Thriller series:
Where the Girls Are Buried   Who Killed the Girls?

Books by AJ Newman and Cliff Deane

Terror in the USA: Virus: – Strain of Islam

These books are available at Amazon:

http://www.amazon.com/-/e/B00HT84V6U

*

Prologue

Most of my novels have a strong central character who is the hero of the story. This novel tells the story of a family that has to deal with a world that has fallen apart and survives in its ashes. The Karr family is the "hero" in this tale, and together they overcome all odds to help each other live through the horrible events that occur during an apocalypse.

Family doesn't always mean blood kin. The Karr family grows stronger as time goes on and with each new member.

Most Post-Apocalyptic stories have the same nuclear bombs, EMPs, and viruses; what makes them unique is how the characters react to the challenges and meet the dangers of a new world as life deals the cards. I hope you find the Karr family's story to be a fresh view on a well-covered genre. I think the story will keep you wondering what's next and how the family will deal with the issues confronting them.

I have sketched out an outline that takes the family through the first year of the apocalypse in four novels. I plan to write those four, and then decide if the family's trials and tribulations merit further story telling.

Enjoy!

AJ Newman

-

Character List

Josephine Karr – She is a Policewoman, Bill's wife and mother to Will, Missy, and Jake.

Bill Karr – He is a Nurse and Josephine's husband.

Will Karr – He is the oldest child at 16.

Missy Karr – She is 15 and a tomboy.

Jake Karr – He is 12 and a couch potato.

Bob Karr – Bill's father and is a widower. He is a retired Army Officer and prepper.

Jane Carter – Josephine's mother. She is a nurse and works with Bill at the local hospital.

Maddie O'Berg – The Senator's daughter. The girl who helps Jane and the Kids, and then joins the Karr Family.

Walt Long – Jo's partner who loves her and wants her to leave Bill and marry him. He is an ex-Army MP.

Barry O'Berg – US Senator from Tennessee. Crooked politician and power hungry sociopath.

Jim Dickerson – Neighbor across the river from the Family's home. The leader of the people resisting O'berg.

*

Cities on Fire:

A Family's Apocalypse

by

AJ Newman

*

Chapter 1

Day One – A Bad Day Gets Worse

They were driving along Algonquin Parkway in Louisville when Walt saw the sign for the Dixie Highway up ahead.

"Let's stop at Al's and get a couple of burgers Doll."

"I could go for a burger," his partner replied.

"Okay, I'll call into the station and tell them."

"Tell Sarge to have you stop calling me Doll."

They had been assigned to patrol the west side of Louisville for six months now and had only run into general domestic disturbances, bicycle thefts, and a few drug busts. They didn't encounter anything that ended up being dangerous or too exciting for that matter. The west end of Louisville was the low-income area of the town and was populated with lower middle class and poor blacks and whites. It had a bad reputation that was much worse than reality.

"Walt, move your hand, or I will break your fingers. I can't drive with you trying to play grab ass all the time."

"I love it when you talk tough like that Jo. It really turns me on."

She slid to a stop in front of Al's, grabbed his hand from her knee, and bent the palm backward until he yelled, "Damn, please let go! That hurts."

"Keep your hands to yourself, or I will report you to the Captain."

"Now wait a minute Jo; you used to love me. We have been partners for three years, and you used to let me touch you."

"Walt that was one time when you got me drunk, and Bill and I were fighting. I didn't know what I was doing, and you act like we were lovers. This has to stop, or I can't be your partner."

His face got red, he tensed up and had to calm himself down before he said anything. He had loved her from the first week he met her. She was five feet four inches tall, a buck twenty and dark brown hair. She had a figure that really turned him on, in her uniform, or wearing street clothes.

"I'm sorry, I couldn't help myself. I promise to be good from now on."

"Seriously, Walt, if you grab me one more time I'm reporting you. I want to be your damn partner, not your lover, and if you can't live with that, then we can't work together."

"I'll be good. Now let's get some burgers."

They walked into Al's and sat in the back with both of them facing the door, a habit that helps to keep Police Officers alive. Germaine, the waiter, came over, took their order, and poured two glasses of water.

"You guys are late tonight. It's 11:00 and the chef went home."

"Germaine, turn the TV to Fox News and tell Al to cook them himself."

"We don't want no stinking FOX News on in this place."

"You give me a rash of shit every day, and you still change the channel to FOX. Why don't you just do it and save the stress for something else in your life," asked Jo?

"Because I like it when yo' face turns that white girl's red. You must have some Injun blood in your family. Now, Walt, there has some Black blood stirring around in his family tree. See that black curly hair; one of my homeboys got in there somehow back in the day."

"Screw you, Germaine. If I wanted my ancestry checked out I'd go to that damn place on TV all of the ti..."

"Walt, shut up. The announcer just said that China has done something wrong to the USA. Shut up and listen."

The FOX anchor said, "We have just received news that the International Money Fund, the United Nations, and the Common market have dropped the US Dollar as the World Currency and switched to the Chinese Yuan. Reports indicate that China has bribed many of the influential leaders of those organizations to force the change. The DOW Jones has plummeted all day due to the speculation and closed over 5,000 points down. Unnamed sources in the Whitehouse tell us that the President will close US trading until further notice to help stabilize the market."

"Bill's Dad has been warning us to buy silver and gold for years. Bill, thought it was stupid. I'm glad I bought over ten thousand Dollars' worth of silver coins five years ago. Silver has tripled in value while gold has only doubled."

"You know me, I'm a prepper. I have silver and gold coins plus enough food, ammo, and guns to start a small country."

"We have a six month's supply of food, but I wish we had bought some ARs and more semi-auto pistols. We only have three shotguns, two lever action 30 30s, and my 9mm Ruger and Keltek. I should have purchased a couple of Glocks and two AR15s."

The TV got much louder just as Germaine brought their burgers, fries, and drinks to them.

"Breaking news! Russia just invaded Belarus, The Ukraine, and the three Balkan countries. They have also placed their ICBMs on alert to launch if any country interferes with their invasion. Jack Terry, the Secretary of State, has logged a complaint with the UN and the President has called President Putin to register a personal complaint on behalf of the countries being invaded."

"Jack, we had eight years of military buildup during the last administration, and now we see this sad state of affairs just three years into Susan Barren's foreign policy disaster."

"General Maddox, what is your take on this situation?"

"We had the Russians and Chinese contained for six years, and now this piss poor excuse of a President has delivered the world to the Commie bast...."

"Sorry, the feed from the General was cut short. We will try to reconnect later in the program."

The announcers continued to analyze the two situations as Jo and Walt ate their burgers and fries.

Jo's phone beeped, and she said, "Time to get our asses back to work."

Jo's father in law, Bob Karr, was an ex-Army Officer who retired after 30 years serving in the 82nd Airborne. He had lived around the Fort Campbell area on and off most of his adult life and settled down in the Middle Tennessee area with his wife. She died the same year Bob retired and left him a lonely man with too much time on his hands. His home, on a small farm, was located a few miles south of Dixon Springs, Tennessee, which was on a piece of land trapped in a loop of the Cumberland River. The area was called the Horseshoe since its shape resembled a horseshoe thanks to the meandering river.

Bob was a staunch conservative and felt that America was falling apart thanks to liberal Democrats. He was proud of what was accomplished during the previous President's two terms to make America strong again; however, the current liberal President destroyed most of that progress. Iran tested a nuclear weapon just two years after her election and had stockpiled ten by the end of her third year in office. Bob had little confidence in the current government or world powers to stop evil in the world.

He purchased the old home and 50 acres to get away from the day-to-day BS in the world. He didn't have a TV much less Cable or an iPhone. He got his daily news from FOX radio.

There were only a few families that lived on this peninsula bounded by the Cumberland River, and he liked it that way. He was friendly to his neighbors but had no real friends.

The bad news that night concerning the change to the Yuan being the world's currency and the Russian invasion scared him. He knew his liberal son wouldn't listen, but he had to try to talk some sense into him. He thought if he failed, he would try talking to his daughter in law. She had a good head on her shoulders.

"Dad, yes I watch the news."

"Son the fucking Ruskies are invading half of Europe. Only nukes will stop the bastards. Come on down here now. When the nukes fly, Louisville will be a war zone in three days."

"Yes, it's bad out there, but I'm not panicking and moving my family to Tennessee. President Barren will somehow handle this mess. The damned Republicans caused this by scaring the Russians and Chinese with our military buildup during the last administration. I hate that clown looking bastard."

Son, you have to list..."

"Dad...Dad...Can I say something? I'm sorry, but I don't think it's the end of the world, and no, we're not coming to the farm. This will blow over as it always does."

"Look, son, I know we don't see eye to eye on politics, but I want you and your family to be safe. The Chinese Yuan is now the world currency. The dollar won't be worth the paper it's printed on, and we will be at war tomorrow. Please bring your family down here to the Horseshoe before the food supply dries up and the riots start."

"Dad, you watch too many of those prepper shows on TV. Look, I love you, and we'll visit at the end of the month. Goodbye."

Bill looked across the desk, saw his friend Dawn, and said, "My old man is off his rocker. He thinks it's the end of the world, the Russians are coming, and my family needs to head down to his farm in Tennessee."

Dawn looked both ways, laid her hand on top of Bill's hand, and said, "Bill, why don't you join me for drinks at my place when we get off. Tell your wife you are pulling a double shift and I can make you forget your troubles."

Bill looked over at the nurse with her cleavage staring him in the face and the tight white slacks and said, "Dawn, that sounds awful good. Let me think about it."

"Bill, I don't want to break up your marriage. We will be friends with benefits."

"So you aren't husband shopping?"

"Hell no. I just want to get you in bed and have some fun."

"You are a brazen hussy."

"Wait until I show you some of my skills in the bedroom."

Bill knew he shouldn't be having this conversation, but he knew Walt had the hots for Jo and Jo wasn't the same anymore toward him. He needed a friend. He looked across the counter, squeezed her hand, and brushed against her as he passed behind her.

"Don't get too greedy at work. There are cameras everywhere and remember your mom in law works here on day shift."

Bill turned red as he said, "I'll meet you in the janitor's closet by Room 203 at 1:00 am sharp and see if you're all talk."

"It's a date."

They walked out of Al's to their patrol car when Walt said, "Jo, something doesn't look right across the street. There is a man in a car with the engine running in front of Patriot Firearms, and another is watching the road from inside the shop. Hell, it's almost midnight they should be closed."

"Damn, you are right. It's a robbery. I'll call it in."

They ducked below the top of the parked cars and went up the street before crossing quickly behind the parked car. The driver must have seen one of them because he honked his horn and pulled closer to the door. He had barely stopped when two masked men came running out of the gun shop with their arms full of weapons.

"Police, stop and raise your hands."

The driver poked a handgun out the window and started blasting away at the two Policemen who had to duck behind a car. This gave the others time to drop their stolen booty into the car's window and come up shooting.

Jo saw a thug's leg below a car, took aim, and shot him just below the kneecap. He was down for the count as his Mac 10 skittered across the street. Walt ran from his hiding spot drawing fire and ducked behind a pickup. One of the robbers moved to get a shot at Walt and exposed himself to Jo's field of fire. She pulled the trigger and shot the man squarely in the chest twice.

The driver honked again for the man in the shop to get in the car, but the man ran to the back of the gun shop. The car sped off with both Jo and Walt taking shots. The car swerved and crashed into a street sweeper that had been abandoned when the gunfire erupted. The driver's head was sticking through the windshield.

"That son of a bitch is going to take hostages, yelled Walt as he saw Jo run up to the door.

Jo crouched down and slowly pushed the door open to reveal one man lying on the floor and another slumped against a display case holding his side with blood everywhere. She cautiously walked into the shop while keeping the display case between her and the back of the store. Walt followed ten feet behind her.

There was complete silence until they heard, "Please don't kill me I have a wife, kids, and grandkids. You can have everything, and I won't press charges."

"Shut the fuck up old man before I cap your fucking ass."

Jo looked up into a mirror and saw the thug holding the owner with a pistol to his head. She looked around the store, and she didn't see any more people just a body to her left.

She whispered, "Walt, cover me. I'm going around the display case. Shoot him when he sees me and turns."

"Be careful."

Jo crawled below the line of sight to the far end of the display case to a position ten feet past the robber who held the owner as a human shield. She slowly rose to an upright stance while keeping the perp in her gun's sights. The man caught a glimpse of her before she could fire and moved the hostage to block her shot.

"Shoot bitch, and you'll kill the old man."

The not so bright criminal forgot that he had turned away from her partner and exposed his side. Walt was twenty feet from the man and decided to go for a body shot. He breathed out, slowly squeezed the trigger with the tip of his finger, and he shot the man in the left arm with the first shot and the side of his chest with the second shot.

Jo took a step forward to make sure the perp wasn't a threat when she heard, "Jo," and then the thunderous sound of several gunshots filled the small room. She felt two extremely painful impacts to her chest. As she fell to the floor, she fired back at the perp who had remained hidden behind a gun safe. One of her bullets hit him in the left eye and blew a large chunk of his skull onto the wall of the gun shop.

The perp got off a wild shot at Walt before Jo shot him and grazed Walt on his left arm below the shoulder. It hurt like hell and Walt held pressure on it while he called in that a policeman was down. He no sooner keyed the mic than he heard their backup arrive. Several policemen came into the shop with guns drawn, searched the back room, and secured the crime scene.

He ran over to Jo and checked to see if she was still alive. She was groggy but still breathing. She was alive because both slugs had hit her body armor.

Two EMTs rushed in, and Walt sent them to Jo first to make sure she was okay. They checked her out, loaded her into the Ambulance along with Walt, and headed to the hospital.

The Lead EMT said, "Thank God the bullets struck her vest. Either one would have probably killed her. Now let me look at your scratch."

The Ambulance arrived at the hospital, and Jo was rushed to the emergency room to check for any serious damage. She started to wake up as they wheeled her through the hallway and asked for her husband.

One of the nurses asked, "How do we find your husband?"

Jo's voice was weak, but she said, "He works here in Emergency. He's Bill Karr."

Bill heard her voice and ran to her side yelling, "That's my wife. What happened? Has she been shot?"

Walt was being examined in the next room. He shoved the Doctor away, walked into the room, and said, "Bill, her body armor stopped both slugs. We stopped a robbery in progress, and one of the bastards was hiding when we thought all of the perps had been accounted for. He shot both of us, but Jo killed him and ended his miserable life."

"Thanks, Walt," Bill replied.

"Mr. Long, get back in your room and let the Doctor stitch you up. Bill, you need to go to the waiting room. You know you shouldn't stay here while we work on your wife."

Bill was holding Jo's hand when she said, "How big was the truck that hit me? My chest hurts. Damn it hurts. Is Walt okay?"

"Yes dear. Your partner only has a minor wound to his arm, and you are going to be back on your feet in a few days."

"Damn this hurts."

The nurse inserted an IV and said, "It won't hurt much longer," as she injected pain medicine into the IV port.

"Bill go! We're taking her to X-ray and then the Doctors will check her out. The body armor took most of the force. We just need to make sure she doesn't have any cracked ribs or soft tissue damage."

"I know, but she's my wife."

"Bill, go sit in the waiting room. Now!

Bob was pissed when his hardheaded liberal son wouldn't listen, so he dialed his daughter-in-law's cell phone number. The phone rang, but Jo didn't answer. He tried a couple of times then decided to call their home number. The phone rang a couple of times, and then he heard, "Hello, this is the Karr residence. May I ask who is calling this late at night?"

"Missy, this is Papaw. Please put your mom on the phone."

"Papaw, I want to talk with you."

"Darling, I'll talk with you later. I'm in a hurry. Please put your mom on the phone."

"Mom is at work."

"Please get Will. Hurry. Please.

"Yes, Papaw."

"Will! It's Papaw. Come to the phone."

Bob could hear Missy yelling for Will, and then Will answered the phone.

"Hey, Papaw, are you watching the news? We stayed up late to see the war. The shit is about to hit the fan."

"Will, this is going to get bad real quick. I tried to talk your hardheaded dad into coming down to the farm before it gets real bad, but he wouldn't listen to me. I'm tryin' to reach your mom."

"Papaw, mom is at work and won't be home until in the morning. I'll let her know to call you."

Bob thought for a few seconds and said, "Son, we'll be at war or attacked sometime in the next few days. If anything happens you know to come down to the farm. Don't you?"

"Papaw, I still have the Bugout bags you gave us for Christmas, and I have added a few things to them. When Mom and Dad get home, I'll try to convince Dad to take us down to the farm."

"Will, remember there is a map to the farm that keeps you off the main highways on your way here in all of the Bugout bags. Use that route if things get bad. I think we will be hit with several EMP bombs first then all out warfare."

"I'll make sure all of our bags are ready and do my best with Dad."

"Son, I love you and Missy and Jake. I wish I were there to bring you down here, but that is your Dad's shot to call. Remember what I taught you and stay safe. Let me talk to Missy and Jake.

"Bill we're taking your wife to her room. She'll be as good as new in a few weeks. She has severe bruising where the bullets struck the vest. She'll be a little drowsy after the pain medicine takes effect, but you can talk to her now. We'll keep her overnight and should release her by noon tomorrow."

"Thanks so much for caring for her. I don't know what I'd do if something bad happened to her."

Walt overheard the conversation and chimed in with, "Bill something bad did happen to her. A perp shot me and shot her twice in the chest. She would be dead now if not for the body armor. I would be dead if she didn't kill the scumbag that was robbing the gun store. We killed or wounded four criminals that our liberal judges keep releasing from jail."

"Walt, I don't want to argue politics. I need to go to my wife's side."

Bill walked away and went to Jo's room. He walked into the room, and his wife was talking with the Captain of her precinct.

"Hello Bill, I'm sorry that Jo had to go through this. Walt's and her quick action saved the owner's life and rid the world of some dangerous people."

Bill glared at the Captain and replied, "Tell that to the dead men's mothers, wives, and children. Killing people isn't always the solution."

Jo replied, "That was uncalled for. Apologize to the Captain."

The Captain was red in the face as he said, "Jo, I'll leave now. Stay home the rest of the week and check in with me after the review board clears the shooting. Thank God, those assholes didn't kill you. Goodbye Mr. Karr."

"Honey I was so...."

"Bill what the hell is wrong with you. Those men killed a man in the store, shot Walt, and tried to kill me, and you spout that liberal bullshit to my Captain. Get the hell out of my room until you promise to apologize to my Captain."

"Honey I was so scared that you might not make it. I'll tell him I'm sorry for yelling at him but not for what I said."

"So you'd rather see them alive and me dead."

"No, I want the guns off the street and out of everyone's hands. Then there wouldn't be all this killing and Cops wouldn't have to execute so many people."

"I can't believe you actually think that outlawing guns would stop criminals from having guns. You are a special kind of stupid. I married an idiot."

"Jo..."

"Don't Jo me. How are the kids doing? I don't want them worried about me."

"I haven't told them anything. They should be sleeping now. I didn't want to call them until I knew how you were doing."

"Bill, please go home and stay with the kids. Now that you have been notified that I was shot they will release my name to the news. I don't want them hearing their mom was shot on the news."

"I'm staying with you besides they'll sleep in until late since it's Friday night. Call your mom to come up and stay with them. She's only a half hour away."

"Okay. I'll call Mom while you call Will."

"Okay, I'll call Will.

"Mom, yes it's me, Jo."

"Are you okay? Josephine, do you know the two policemen who were shot?"

"Yes Mom, it was my partner and me. We are okay. My body armor stopped the bullets, and Walt only got a scratch."

"Oh, my God. Are you really okay?"

"Yes, Mom. Can you go stay with the kids until I am released tomorrow?"

"I thought you were okay."

"I just have some bruising. They are keeping me until tomorrow as a safety precaution."

"I'm a nurse, and that could mean a lot of things and several are bad."

"Mom, Bill is here and he agrees with what we were told. I'll be home tomorrow and take a week off then go back to work. Bill is calling Will now to make sure they don't hear it first on the news."

"How is Bill handling the situation?"

"Not well. He thinks Walt and I executed some poor misdirected family men."

"Darling, I will keep my comments to myself. I'm not a conservative at all, but you know Bill is full of liberal crap. You knew it when you were dating him. Your Dad didn't like him, and I can barely have a conversation with him. I'll stay with the kids. I'll gather some things and leave now."

"Thanks, Mom. I'm getting a little drowsy. I'll try to call the kids later."

"Will this is Dad."

"Dad I know who you are. Have you been watching the news? Dad, the Russians have invaded the Balkan countries and are racing into Poland. We are at war. Please come home and let's go to Papaws."

"Son I need you to focus on what I am going to tell you. Your Mom is in the hospital, and she is okay. She only has some bruises. She is fine. I just wanted to make sure you all know she wasn't hurt in the robbery."

"What robbery? I've had the TV on FOX news and haven't seen the local news."

"Your Mom and partner broke up a robbery and were shot at by the robbers. Her body armor stopped the bullets. I need you to be calm when I ask you to get your brother and sister on the phone, and your Grandma is coming to stay with you tonight until we get home after lunch tomorrow."

"Wow, mom got shot. I'll bring Missy and Jake to see Mom."

"No. Let them sleep. She is sleeping, and it's not really a big deal. She has some pain, but we are just keeping her here overnight as a precaution per our rules."

"Dad, Missy, and I are awake and watching FOX News. Jake is asleep in his room. I'll tell Missy and let Jake sleep."

"Your Grandma should be there in an hour or so to take care of you until we get home."

Jane arrived at her daughter's home on the east side of Louisville, parked the car, and walked toward the front door, rang the doorbell, and Will came to the door and gave her a hug.

"Grandma, I'm glad to see you. Missy is taking this hard. She is worried about Mom. Thanks for comin'."

"Take me to her and place my bag in the guest room. Where's Jake?"

"He's up in his room asleep."

Missy was glad to see her Grandma and was soon calmed down and talking rationally. Will went back to the family room and saw a breaking news report had just started.

"FOX News has just learned that German and US main battle tanks are engaged in a desperate fight to stop the Russian tanks from rolling across Poland. British and French warplanes have joined the German and US aircraft in another major fight for air superiority over Polish skies."

"Frank we have video from a Polish student. Roll the footage. This was shot a few miles east of Warsaw."

The short video played for a few seconds and then went blank.

"Viewers the video was poor quality; however, you saw a German tank explode and Apache helicopters firing missiles at Russian tanks in the distance. Early reports confirm that Russia has fifty armored divisions attacking all along the western border of the Common Market countries. President Barren ordered the US forces to retreat and stand down, but the US Command has not complied with the order and has bombed several Russian military bases. I have unconfirmed word that hundreds of cruise missiles have been fired at Russia and that the US Air Defense has shot most of the Russian missiles out of the air."

"Brett, my Pentagon source just told me that our military has joined Japan, Korea, India, and Israel in major attacks against the Chinese and Russian forces. This is the start of World War III. The President is not in control of our military."

"Frank, I don't know who is in charge, but anyone could do a better job than President Warren."

"Joan, have any nuclear bombs been deployed yet?"

"No, but I expect this at any minute. Viewers while we don't have any word from Homeland Defense, I expect them or the President to address the nation at any moment."

"Viewers, be prepared to run to your basements or bomb shelters. ICBMs could be launched any minute."

The phone rang, and it was Papaw Bob on the phone.

"Papaw, the shit has hit the fan. Mom is in the hospital, and Grandma is staying with us."

"Where is your Dad? What happened?"

"He's at the hospital with Mom. She was shot, but her vest stopped the bullets. She will be okay. I don't know what to do. I think we should be with you on the farm, but I don't want to leave without Mom and Dad."

"Son, do you have a car at the house?"

"Yes, my Explorer, and Grandma's Buick."

"Let me speak to Jane."

"I'll get her."

"Grandma! Papaw wants you on the phone."

"Bob, how are you doing?"

"Jane, I'm okay, and I'm sorry to hear about Jo's situation, but she is a tough woman and will be fine. Jane, do you know what is happening in Europe?"

"Yes, and it is scaring the crap out of me. What do you think we need to do?"

"I tried to talk my hardheaded son into bringing the kids down here, and he laughed at me. Jane, nuclear-tipped missiles will be exchanged by both sides in the next few days. You need to load up the kids and bring them down here now. Will knows what to pack, but the key is to bring food, guns, and ammo. I have a river nearby, so water is not a worry. Will knows the way. I'll call Bill, and you call Jo. We must convince them to check her out of the hospital and get their asses down here ASAP."

Is it really that bad? It's 2:30 in the morning. Oh my, the kids are still up."

"Yes, it is that bad."

"I'll have Will start loading up his Explorer while I call Jo. We will call you when we hit the Tennessee border."

"Jane, Will knows the family Bugout plan. Ask him to go over it with you on the way. Make sure you have plenty of food, weapons, and water in the truck for the trip. I'll try to catch Bill again. Good luck."

"Mom, I'm okay. Don't worry."

"Darling, listen. Bill told me you are okay. The USA is at war with Russia and China. I'm taking the kids down to Tennessee to stay at Bob's home until this is over or the world ends. Tell your stupid husband to check you out of the hospital and go to Tennessee right now. Jo this is the big one your father always warned us about."

"Mom, are you sure?"

"Yes, turn the news on while you get dressed. The USA is in a land war with Russia in Europe. We have bombed Russian military and have shot down over a hundred of their planes and destroyed about 200 of their tanks. We're leaving in an hour. Goodbye. We'll see you at Bob's house. I love you."

"Bye Mom I love you too."

"Nurse, get my husband in here now," Jo demanded as the pain medicine kicked in. Her words were now being slurred, and she was drowsy as Bill entered her room.

"Bill, we need. Oh shiiiit. Weee nee.... Bob...." She said as she slumped over in a deep sleep. The trauma along with the pain medication finally took their toll, and she was out for the night.

The phone went to voice mail for the fourth time, and Bob said, "Damn it Bill answer my call. Get Jo and come on down. Nukes will be flying soon. The kids are on their way down."

Bill was surprised to see Walt still in the waiting room as he passed by on his way back to Jo's room. Walt looked up and said, "Bill, how is she doing?"

"Walt, I know you are concerned, but you can go home now. She is in good hands. I thought that you would be in a bomb shelter somewhere with this new war going on today."

"Bill, quite frankly I should be out of Louisville and somewhere much safer, but Jo is my partner, and I can't leave her. You should be taking your wife and kids to your Dad's farm before the shit hits the fan."

"You're just as bad as my Dad with this end of the world as we know it crap. The President will do something tonight to appease the Russians, and this will blow over. It always does."

"Sticking your head in the sand won't make this go away. The Russians are losing now that all of Europe and the USA have bombed all of their airbases and our A10s and Apaches have blown their tanks into burning hulks. They won't give up. They will nuke us, and we will nuke them. Everyone loses in the end. Get your ass out of town before the riots start and the grid goes down."

"Walt, you and my Dad are fools. Go home. You can't see Jo; she's asleep.

Dawn walked up to the Nursing Station and saw Bill walking away from a man who was yelling at him. She waited until he was close and asked, "Bill, who is that and why is he mad at you?'

"It's my wife's partner, and he is one of those assholes who always think it's going to be doomsday any minute," he replied while lowering his voice.

"He's probably sleeping with Jo. He's like a puppy dog in the waiting room all worried about my wife. I know something is going on," Bill moaned.

Bill didn't notice that Walt was spying on Dawn and him from behind the door to the waiting room. Bill stroked Dawn's hand when the other Nurse turned her back, and he pointed down the hall towards the janitor's closet. She left first then he followed behind her. Walt saw them duck into the closet and knew what was going on behind that door.

Walt traveled over to Jo's room, sat in the chair beside her bed, and watched her sleep. He had fallen in love with her the first week they worked together. She was beautiful, had a great sense of humor, and was very smart. She was also very brave and at times tried to prove herself too much. He had told her on several occasions that she was as good and any man on the force, but she always tried to prove that she was as good as a man.

He held her hand as she slept and lost track of time. A short while later he felt a hand on his as it ripped her hand from his.

"That's my wife's hand, and you need to remember you are her partner, not her boyfriend! Get the hell out of my wife's room."

Dawn and the other nurse heard the commotion and ran to the room in time to hear the last part of the exchange between the two angry men.

"Bill, Jo is my partner and yes I am worried about her. You should be more concerned about her than this blonde nurse you were playin' with in the broom closet."

"I'll..."

"You won't do a damn thing but zip up your pants and wipe the lipstick off your cheek before Jo wakes up and sees the evidence. You don't deserve a woman like Jo."

Bill wiped at his cheek as he replied, "Get him out of here!"

Two security guards ran up to the argument, and one said, "Walt, what's going on?"

"Nothing but an upset husband. His wife was shot today while he's banging a nurse here."

"Walt, come on with us. We don't need more of a scene than what has already happened."

Walt complied and left with the security guards. He apologized to them as he left but didn't tell them what Bill was doing with Dawn.

"Grandma I loaded our Bugout Bags, my pistol, rifle, shotgun, food, and water. Missy packed clothes for all of us and a first aid kit into the Explorer. I left Mom's guns, Dad's and her Bugout Bags that Papaw gave them. I left a note on the kitchen counter telling them where we went. Anything else you want me to do?"

"No. Great job son. Jake, you and Missy, sit in the back, and I will drive while your brother navigates for us."

Jane started the Explorer, left the subdivision, and drove to Highway 60 East. She quickly got on Highway 264 heading southwest so she could get on Highway 65 South.

"Grandma, look to your right. There are several big fires," Missy said.

Will replied, "The looting and rioting are now beginning, and the electricity is still on. Imagine how bad it will get when the power goes off."

"Will, don't scare the kids. Let's think good thoughts and travel south as fast as we can."

"Sorry, Grandma. Hey, there's our ramp up ahead."

Jane got off Highway 264 and made the turn down to the loop that placed them on Highway 65 South. She looked back at Louisville and saw several large fires in the review mirror. She silently thanked God that she was out of there and taking the kids to safety. She couldn't help but worry about her daughter and son in law, but she knew Jo would get his sorry ass on the road and down to Tennessee.

"Grandma, Will asked, "Do you think we will ever be able to go golfing again? I liked going with you and Grandpa."

"Son, you, and I will definitely go golfing again even if we have to mow the whole 18 holes ourselves.

Kids, I'm stopping at my home to pick up some clothes and personal items. It should be safe but keep your eyes out for any problems."

She got off at the Clermont exit and headed East on Highway 245 until she saw the road to her house. She pulled up in front of the house and got out of the Explorer.

"Kids stay in the car. I'll be right back."

Will looked at his iPhone and saw that it was 5:45 am, and wondered how the night had flown by so fast.

Walt got into his patrol car and pulled out of the driveway to go home to his apartment. He knew he should gather his stuff and head up to Kentucky. He thought about Jo and pulled off the highway south of the airport. He was deep in thought and fell asleep.

*

Chapter 2

Day One - TSHTF

"Bill, you son of a bitch. It's 5:30 and we should be on the way to your Dad's by now. The kids are probably halfway there."

"What? Who told them to go to Dad's place?"

"I did. Turn the news on. The entire world is at war. We need to get out of here and get our butts down to Tennessee."

Jo pulled the IV out of her arm and grabbed her clothes out of the closet.

"Jo, you need to rest."

"Where are my gun and holster?"

"Your Captain took your gun because of department regulations since it was involved in a shooting."

"Thank God Walt put my back up gun in my purse," Jo said as she tucked the Keltek P11 9mm into her waistband in the middle of her back.

"Come on. We need to roll."

"Jo, wait."

"Look, Bill, I'm going home to get some things and heading south to your Dad's; you can stay here or come with me if you stay here don't ever come back again."

She walked down the hall brushing the nurses off and headed to the elevator with Bill trying to catch up to her. He jumped into the elevator just before the door closed. The ride down was filled with silence, and as soon as the door opened, she bolted for the lobby doors.

"Bill where are you parked?"

"Over in the west parking lot. Follow me."

The sun was barely above the skyline in the east, and the traffic on all of the streets was building up when there was silence. Every car and truck had died, which resulted in numerous crashes. The Hospitals air conditioning motors wound down and stopped. There was complete silence then they heard people yelling and cursing at each other.

A thunderous explosion rocked them from behind, and they turned to see half of the east wing of the hospital disappear into a fireball and smoke. Jo dove for cover under a car and yelled at Bill to join her. Bill stood there with his mouth gapped open and a dumb look on his face.

"What the fuck was that," screamed Jo as she scanned the area.

There were other explosions all around them, but not close enough that they could see anything. Then there was a roar as something overhead roared past them. A 747 flew just a few feet over them and crashed a block away into an apartment complex, which became a ball of fire.

Jo looked at the parking lot and saw scores of people with bloody head wounds, arms dangling at odd angles, and carrying injured children walking toward the hospital.

Bill saw the injured and said, "I have to go help these people. I'll be home later."

"Bill, we have three kids that need us. Come with me, or you will never see me again."

"But, but what happened. I can't deal with this. Why did this happen?"

Bill continued jabbering on and on about this wasn't supposed to happen and the President said they were safe.

Jo couldn't take any more of his whining and slapped him as she yelled, "Bill, get a grip. We have three kids who need us to be adults and help them make it through this disaster. Put your big girl panties on and get moving you wussie."

Jo started walking east in the direction of their house, and her husband followed her in a daze. His whole world was shattered and nothing made sense.

The entire city was a maze of crashed and stalled vehicles. There were black columns of smoke rising in all directions, and people were milling around in their yards and in shopping mall parking lots.

The city of Louisville had dozens of major fires caused by fallen aircraft and vehicle crashes. A dump truck crashed into a gasoline tanker on the bridge to New Albany, and the entire bridge was on fire. Their city was on fire, and most of the residents didn't have a clue what had turned their lives upside down. Most would die over the next three months.

The crashed airplanes, wrecked cars, and heart attacks resulted in thousands of injured and dying citizens scattered around the city. Several people asked Jo to stop and help them, and it took three times before she realized that she had her police uniform on.

Bill and she stopped and helped free several people from car wrecks and placed a tourniquet on one man's leg when Jo took off the police shirt and tied it around her waist. She knew her first job was to get home and find her kids, and then they had to go to Bob's home in Tennessee.

She only had her pants and a sports bra on, which allowed her to be invisible to most of the injured people. She knew she would never get to her kids if she kept stopping. She had to keep after her husband to force him to keep walking past people she was sworn to protect. This hurt her deep inside, but she kept picturing one of her kids needing help. They moved on as fast as she could push Bill who was in a daze.

They had covered about twenty blocks when Jo recognized Al's restaurant up ahead and Patriot Arms across the street. She stopped and put her shirt back on and tucked it neatly into her pants.

"Bill, we're going gun shopping."

An explosion nearby woke Walt up as it caused the patrol car to rock and shake. Debris hit the roof of the car and shattered the back window. Walt opened the door, staggered out and onto his feet to see a plane falling out of the sky and crash into the airport terminal. Walt keyed the mic on his walkie-talkie and found the radio was dead. He reached into the patrol car, grabbed the mic and it was dead also.

He jumped into the driver's seat to head over to the crash, and the key turned, but the car didn't crank. While he was doing this, several other airplanes crashed. He got out of the car and saw that hundreds of vehicles had crashed or stalled in the streets.

He checked his phone for the time, and the screen was black. He tried turning the device on to no avail.

"Holy shit; there's been a nuke or EMP blast. Everything is dead," he yelled to himself.

Walt started walking to his apartment, which was a mile away and only a block from Al's restaurant. People tried to stop him for help or to ask him what had happened. Walt was in shock and didn't reply; he just walked on past them with a blank look on his face.

Jane only took 15 minutes to gather her things, but she took the time to shut off the gas and electricity to the house before walking out to the Explorer. It was now daylight, and she saw the trails for jets in the air. Louisville Airport was busy this time of the morning with Fed-X, UPS, and passenger flights vying to get airborne.

She was surprised when the Explorer's lights went dark. The entire city's lights went out a second afterward. Her home was only a few blocks from the highway, and she noticed the roar of the traffic had ceased.

Suddenly there was an explosion east of the airport then another south of her home.

"Grandma, nothing works. My phone and game went dead," Missy yelled.

"My iPhone is dead."

Will turned the key to start his Explorer and nothing happened.

"Grandma, my truck is also dead. There has either been a nuclear EMP, that's an Electro Magnetic Pulse or a major Solar Flare. Those are the only two things that destroy all electronics."

"What do we do now?"

"Grandma, we can do one of three things. We can find an old car without electronics that should run. We can ride bikes, or we can walk."

"Oh dear, I don't know where to find such a car, but I have three bicycles in the garage. Will, please take Missy to fetch the bikes. There is a hand pump hanging on the wall above the workbench if you need it to air up the tires. Let Jake sleep a while more."

They found the bikes and all three needed some air, so Missy and Will took turns pumping until the tires were filled. Will also took tools from his Grampa's tool chest that he thought could be needed for bike repair. He then searched through mounds of car and bicycle parts to find a tube patch kit and a spare inner tube for the bikes. They were all the old-style cruiser bikes, and all had 26-inch tires.

"Now we need to see what we need to leave behind. I don't think we can pack everything on the bicycles."

Will took his gramps old bike, wired a plastic tote to the front fender and handlebars, and filled it with food, water and his change of clothes. He strapped his Bugout bag on his back. He would tote Jake on the book rack on top of the back fender.

"Son I have this old map that your Gramps and I used to use to find our way down to your great Uncle Tom's in Lebanon, Tennessee. It looks like we can take back roads to Glasgow and then keep on back roads all the way to Bob's farm. I think it's best to avoid the large cities."

"Grandma, I agree. Papaw has taught me a lot about survival, and I also read Post-Apocalyptic Science Fiction, and the large cities will be the first big problems as the looting and riots begin. We must get as far as possible during the first two to three days before the food runs out. After that people will kill us for our bikes or a scrap of food."

Will kept his Ruger MKII .22 strapped to his side under his shirt and his 12 Gauge shotgun on top of the tote. Jane took the Winchester .30 .30 and placed it on top of the handlebar basket that contained more food and water. Her bike had wire baskets on both sides of the rear tire, and those were filled with a plastic tarp and survival gear. Missy's bike was her Mom's old bike, and it didn't have any baskets, so she only had her Bugout bag strapped on her back and a bag of clothes tied to the handlebars.

"Son, don't forget the bicycle pump."

"Got it wired to the frame."

Jane waved bye to her house, Jake climbed on the back of Will's bike, and they rode off on their trip to Tennessee.

Jo walked up to the front door, which had a closed sign behind the glass and rapped her knuckles on the door several times. After the fourth time, a young man came to the door and yelled, "We're closed."

Jo showed the man her badge and asked him to open the door. He opened it enough to talk and said, "Officer, we're closed. There's going to be looting and rioting sometime today, and we're moving most of our inventory to a safer location."

"I need to talk to the owner."

"My Dad is in the back. He had a rough day yesterday and doesn't feel like talking."

Jo stuck her index finger into one of the bullet holes in her shirt and said, "Me too. I was one of the officers who stopped the robbery. I just wanted to check on your Dad."

"Dad, come up front."

The older man walked to the front, saw Jo, and said, "You're the lady cop who killed that asshole and saved my life. Is this the other cop?"

"No, that's my husband."

"Officer Karr I owe you my life. What are you doing out here walking? You know the whole city's electrical grid, cars, and phones are dead, don't you?"

"Yes, I was just leaving the hospital when the shit hit the fan and found our car was dead. Our home is in East Louisville, so we started walking."

"How bad were you hurt?"

"I'm okay. The bulletproof vest stopped the bullets. I'm very sore but will be fine. My partner got a flesh wound but is okay and was released yesterday."

"Thank God you both are okay."

"Sir I need a big favor. I don't think the power is coming back on for a while and the criminals will be killing, raping and looting soon. We're heading to a safe place south of here, and I need to buy or borrow a pistol from you. The department took my service Glock to complete the shooting investigation."

"Come on in. I owe you my life, and you are right; the world won't return to normal for years. You need more than a pistol. We will equip you and give you a ride out of the city."

"Dad, we don't know her."

"Son she saved my life, and I'm going to make sure she has a fighting chance to get to her safe place. Now, Ben go get two backpacks and fill them up with our standard survival gear, MREs, and two canteens. Make sure you have two Life Straws in each bag. Now my friend what guns do you want."

"Sir...."

38

"Call me Shorty. All my friends do."

"Shorty, I only have a couple of hundred dollars on me...."

"Look, your money is no good here. What do you need? Just ask, and it's yours. How about two Glock 17s, a Keltek Sub 2000 and a Bushmaster AR15 to start with? That gives you three weapons that use the same 9mm ammo and magazines and a rifle that can reach out and touch the bad guys. I'll add four loaded mags per gun, 250 rounds of 9mm, and 250 .223s. That's a bit of weight, but you may be fighting for your lives. Ben, add two tactical vests to carry the magazines and Glocks."

"Shorty I can't thank you enough."

"Woman you saved my life. I would do anything for you."

"Jo, I won't need any guns," Bill said.

"Shut up; they are not for you. You'll pack my spares. I'm sorry Shorty, but my husband is one of those liberals who doesn't like guns."

"Sonny, you'd better listen to your wife. She's going to need you to back her up like her partner did the other day. They saved my life and each other's lives when those scumbags tried to kill us all."

Shorty brought two holsters with the Glocks and two 17 round magazines already in the holster. Jo made Bill strap his on and then put hers around her waist. Ben had installed shoulder straps on both rifles and the guns were ready to go.

Jo said, "Bill I know you don't like guns, but trust me you will be shot at and shoot back at someone trying to rob or kill us this week so listen."

She then showed him how to load, handle, and fire the Glock and the Sub 2000. He was like a man handling a rattlesnake for the first time.

"Look I know you don't like this, but you could be saving one of our kid's life with one of those guns so get over the bullshit and be prepared to shoot."

Ben brought the backpacks to the back of the store along with the tactical vests and other gear.

Shorty came back from the front and said, "Ben you and Ralph stay here while George and I take them to their house and then to the south side of the city so they can start their trip south. After we drop them off, we'll drop the first load off at the ranch and get back here ASAP. I figure we have until dark to be out of here. Then the shit really hits the fan."

Shorty took them by their home and waited for them to gather what they needed for their trip, which wasn't much since Shorty had equipped them so well. Jo hid the family pictures, her jewelry, and other precious keepsakes in their safe under the garage floor, which was masked by a set of shelves. She took a bag of silver coins and twenty gold coins with them to trade or purchase with later. She placed the silver coins in two money belts with the coins spaced out around their waists to keep them hidden.

Bill went to the back of the garage and retrieved a baby carriage built for a runner to push as he ran. He used to push the kids along as he ran when they were babies.

He placed a case of pint water bottles, cans of meat and a small hiker's tent in the carriage and pushed it to the truck.

"Jo, I pushed the kids in this, and we can use it to help takes some of the load off."

"Great idea honey. Let's go."

Shorty looked at them and said, "I wish I had an old car to give you. You two look like you're going to run a marathon."

"We run 50 milers five times a year and train three times a week. This will be three of them in three to five days if we don't find transportation."

"No shit. You are going to run down to Tennessee."

"Yes."

"Won't you attract attention with a carbine and an AR strapped to your backs."

"They'll go in the baby buggy until we need them."

The truck pulled out, and Jo looked back at their two story home and wondered if she would ever see it again. Bill looked toward the hospital and wondered if he'd ever see Dawn again and if she was as good in bed as she claimed. He went into the closet yesterday, but couldn't make love to Dawn with his wife in the hospital.

Shorty dropped them off at the intersection of Highway 265 and Highway 61 and bid them goodbye.

Walt walked back to the hospital to see if he could find Jo and talk her into heading up to Kentucky. One end of the Hospital was engulfed in fire and had collapsed. He entered the Emergency entrance and made his way through a tangled mess of Doctors and Nurses trying to care for hundreds of wounded people.

He arrived at the room Jo had been in and found the room empty. He started to leave when he heard a noise.

"Jo left with her husband," the Nurse Dawn blubbered between long crying spells.

"How long ago did they leave?"

"Sniff. About half an hour ago. I can't believe Bill left with his bitch wife."

Walt looked at the beautiful young thing and thought what the heck. I can't have Jo today so Dawn will do. He helped her up off the floor and to a patient's room. He calmed her down and started unbuttoning her dress when she realized what was happening she said, "Stop. I'm going home."

Walt drew his pistol, stuck it against her temple, and said," If you want to ever go home again you'll get your clothes off and do what I say when I say."

"Screw you. I'm going home."

Walt hit her on the neck with the butt of the gun, and she said, "Don't hurt me. I'll do it."

She and Walt undressed. He got what he wanted and left her crying on the bed.

As he left he said, "If you see that wimp Bill, tell him I'm going to take Jo and kill his sorry ass."

He left the poor girl crying and never realized that he had become the criminal that he had fought half of his adult life. He hated everybody and was in a rage that blinded him from reason.

Will thought the ride was much more difficult due to the stalled and crashed cars littering the highway. He wished people had pulled over to the side instead of stopping in the middle of the highway. Most people were still milling around their cars without a clue what had happened. At first, no one paid attention to them but as the day wore on several tried to get them to stop. A few offered to buy the bicycles. One man screamed at them and threw rocks as they whizzed by him.

The people appeared to be waiting for the police to come and sort things out and then call them a tow truck. Will was very thankful that his Papaw and Mom had warned him about the possibility of this happening. They had given him instructions on how to handle himself and what he should do when TEOTWAWKI occurred. He doubted that most of these people had a clue what to do when the end of the world as we know it occurred.

Will saw the man blocking their path ahead first and yelled back, "Trouble ahead. Wait and follow me when I cut across to the other side of the road."

The man started waving as they got within 100 feet and yelled for them to stop. Will cut to his right quickly with the others following and they soon left the man behind them.

Earlier they had made the mistake of stopping for a woman a few miles out of Clermont, and two men jumped out of the bushes to take their bikes. Will drew his pistol and fired a shot into the ground, and they backed off allowing the family to escape. They wouldn't make that mistake again.

Jane watched the next hill up ahead get closer as they zoomed down a long winding hill that took them to a valley and a stream at the bottom. They built up as much speed as safely possible to give them momentum up the next hill. Jane had driven this road dozens of time and never thought about having to push a bicycle up a hill a mile long.

They shifted down several gears and strained to keep the bikes moving. Jane's legs grew exhausted first, and then Will's and finally Missy's legs were exhausted. Will would normally make it to the top of a hill such as lay in front of him, but Jake was 80 pounds of dead weight added to the fifty pounds of water, food, and supplies. They were all now walking to the top of the hill in slow motion. Jake at least helped push the bike between complaints and the constant, "When are we going to get there," comments.

"Grandma, I'm tired," whined Jake.

"Okay, we've been riding for over four hours, and it's time to take a break and have some lunch. Let's pull off the road into those bushes and hide."

They pushed their bikes through the weeds into a stand of trees and bushes, which hid them from the road.

Will, where are we? I think that is Elizabethtown up ahead."

Will was already examining the map and replied, "Yes Elizabethtown is a mile ahead. We're only averaging five miles per hour thanks to stopping to rest and walking up the hills. That means it will take 32 hours to get to Papaws if we rode straight through. My guess is that we can only ride for 10 hours a day, so that puts us at Papaws on Tuesday morning if nothing bad happens."

"That matches my guess. A simple four-hour drive now takes eight times as long. Everybody drink plenty of water and eat those energy bars. We'll rest for an hour and then swing wide around Elizabethtown. The stalled cars and wrecks will be worse as we go around E-town."

"We need to flex our legs as we rest to help avoid cramps or them getting stiff. In three days we will have muscles in our legs that will make these hills look like bumps."

Missy threw a pinecone at him and said, "I'm a girl. I don't want to look like the Hulk."

"Grandma, look at the map. I think we cut off Highway 65 when we get to the Hodgenville Road overpass, take it down to Hodgenville, and then take Highway 31E down to Glasgow. That's the way Papaw said to go."

"Good job Will. That's the way Grampa and I traveled to Tennessee many times long ago."

"Shake a leg kids. Time to get moving."

"Grandma, what does shake a leg even mean?"

"It means to get you butt in gear, or I'll tan your tail. At least that's what my Grandfather always told me."

They rode until Will stopped them at the Hodgenville Road overpass and pushed their bikes down the hill to the road below. This road took them through an industrial area on the east side of the city, and they only saw a few people.

One man gave them thumbs up and yelled, "Get the Hell out of Dodge and to your Bugout location."

Will and Jane gave him thumbs up and kept pedaling away from the city. An hour later, they were out of the suburbs and back in the country. Papaw had told Will many times that the first day was the best to travel because most people wouldn't have a clue what happened. Then every day afterward got more dangerous and that after three days one should hold up for a month and let everyone kill each other or starve to death while you stay hidden.

They cut over to Highway 61 a few miles north of Hodgenville, went around the city to Highway 31E, and headed south. They were a mile out of the city when they stopped to rest after pulling off the road and hiding in a clump of bushes.

They were taking a ten-minute break when they heard a vehicle approaching from the north. The vehicle stopped on the road not far from them, and two young men got out of the ATV.

"Shit, they had to go this way. How did we lose 'em? Henry wanted them there bicycles."

"Maybe they cut off on one of those side roads back a piece."

"Let's go!"

The ATV took off and was out of sight quickly.

45

"Children we were lucky those men didn't find us. A few people must have figured out their cars are worthless. Let's move on quickly and keep an eye on your mirrors for vehicles coming up from behind. If we see anyone that looks like a threat we will get off the road and hide."

"Grandma, I'll give Jake my binoculars to scan ahead of us, and I'll stop and look before we go over the top of any hills."

"Great. Everyone keep your eyes peeled and yell if you see anything. Remember to look in your mirrors."

They had been riding for over eight hours when they stopped for their next rest, and as usual, they hid off the side on the road. The road was somewhat flatter, and they covered over sixty miles since leaving Jane's home that morning. They were now about a mile north of Glasgow and hid their bike behind an old barn while they rested and ate supper.

"Kids, I plan for us to rest for a half hour and then try to ride another three to four hours, so we will be safely south of Glasgow before nightfall. Are you up to it?"

Will replied, "Missy, I know that you are beat, but we have to get as close to Papaws as possible today. There will be more danger every day after today. You can do it."

"Grandma, I'll do my best, but I will need more breaks to rest."

"That's my girl. Now you kids take a short nap while Granny keeps a lookout."

Will motioned for her to move away from the other two and then said, "Grandma, please take a nap and let me keep look out. You need the rest more than me."

"Son you have been packing Jake for over eight hours."

"I'm a long distance runner in high school. Dad got that one thing right. Jake, Missy, and I run with Mom and Dad almost every day. I'm tired, but I have a lot of gas still left in me. Take a nap. Please."

"Thanks, I'm exhausted."

Will looked at his watch, saw it was only 4:15, and knew they had only another three hours or so of daylight. He watched the highway and noticed that most people had abandoned their cars and had walked to the nearest town to seek help. He checked the map and chose a place to spend the night. He picked a place close to where the Cumberland Parkway crossed Highway 31E. There was a bridge over a stream a few hundred feet from the Highway 31E overpass that would make a great place to spend the night and keep hidden from people passing by.

They rested for the half hour, and then Will woke them up and told them to massage each other's legs before getting on their bikes.

Jake said, "My legs are fine. Could you massage my butt? The bars hurt even with the padding you wrapped around them."

Will swatted him on his behind and said, "That's the only massage you're going to get today. Let's hit the road."

The trip around Glasgow was exhausting and sapped their remaining energy even though they stopped a couple of times for short rest breaks. After three more hours, they were only a mile from the intersection where Will planned to hide and spend the night.

Missy pointed to some people milling around in a parking lot by a hotel and said, "They're having a party. Look they have a grill and people are dancing."

Will yelled back to her, "Just hope they don't see us."

"Too late one of the men waved at us."

"Pick up the pace we need to get away from here quick. Pump those pedals."

It was almost dark when they arrived at the Highway 31E intersection. Will kept looking back, didn't see anyone following, and then decided to go ahead and stop under the overpass by the creek. They walked their bikes down the slope from the highway to the bridge over the creek and placed them up under the bridge so no one could see them from the bridge. They talked for a few minutes and then Missy and Jake lay down and were asleep in a few minutes.

"Will, I'll take the first watch since I got to nap earlier today. I'll wake you up in two hours, and we'll rotate every two hours."

"That will work. Here's my watch. Goodnight."

Will was fast asleep the minute his head rested on his Bugout Bag. Jane stayed on her feet for about 15 minutes then sat down on the concrete retaining wall as she fought off sleep. She leaned back against the bridge abutment and was fast asleep. The family was worn out, and a bomb would not have made them stir. Certainly, the three men stealing their bikes and Will's shotgun weren't noticed either.

They didn't hear the men walking through the brush coming to steal their bikes. The young men were half-drunk and just wanted the bikes to help them go home to Nashville. They made a lot of noise crashing down the hill to get to the bikes under the bridge. Each one took one of the bikes and was about to leave when one saw the shotgun leaning against the bridge abutment next to Jane. He giggled while he took it away from the guard while she slept.

Jane didn't hear the girl yelling at the men to stop or hear her throw rocks at them to run them off either. One was about to steal Will's rifle and Jake's Bugout Bag when she chucked a rock and hit him on the back of his head. The one with the shotgun ran over to the girl and hit her on the head with the butt end. The blow knocked her unconscious, and she fell down between Jake and Will.

Missy opened her eyes, thought she was dreaming and went back to sleep. Jake moaned and never woke up until morning. Will was dreaming about whatever young boys his age dreamed about and slept through the night.

The men took their bikes and left as quickly as possible into the night. One of them left a trail of blood from a large gash on his head.

*

Chapter 3

Day One – Aftermath

"Pop, come here. Sumthin' bad is happening."

"Hold your damn horses. I'll be there when I get there."

Jim Dickerson was a mountain of a man. He stood six foot four in his stocking feet and weighed a tad over 280 pounds, yet he moved with the grace of a dancer. He had the largest farm in Wilson County Tennessee and was a man to be reckoned within County and State politics. He had been up since the crack of dawn reading his Bible then watching the Ag News Channel in order to stay caught up on any new developments in farming.

Jim was pissed that his TV went off when the power went off a few minutes ago, and he was headed to the laundry room to see if a circuit breaker had tripped. He traveled half way to the fuse panel when he heard his son, Hoss, yelling for him to go outside.

He walked out the back door onto the large deck and said, "What's going on that you have to be yellin' at the top of your fool lungs?"

"Pop, look north Nashville. An airplane crashed over there north of Nashville."

Just as he finished there was an explosion a few miles due west over by Lebanon and Hoss said, "Terrorist are bombing us."

There was a roar overhead, and they saw a large jet a few hundred feet above them heading to the ground.

"Hoss, that plane is trying to land, and it's engines are dead. Go get my truck and some fire extinguishers from the pole barn. We have to help them. I'll get the fire extinguishers from the house."

Hoss ran back from the barn with two fire extinguishers but no truck, so Jim said, "Did you forget the truck?"

"No Pop. Your truck wouldn't start and mine's dead also."

"Do what? I'll have to see this myself," Jim said as he walked past his son on the way to the barn.

Just as Hoss said, neither of the trucks would start. Jim saw his Gator parked in front of the barn and tried to start it without success.

"Hoss call the Sheriff and report the crash."

Hoss fished his phone out of his pocket and saw a black screen. He tried to turn the phone on, and nothing happened.

"Pop, it's dead."

"The powers off, our trucks won't start, airplanes are falling from the sky and phones don't work; we've either had a big assed Solar Flare or attacked with a nuclear EMP. Go get my '49 FI out of the garage, and we'll go to the crash."

"Pop, it won't start if a new truck won't...."

"Just do as I say, or I'll box your ears."

Hoss quickly left to get the old truck. Hoss was four inches taller and 50 pounds heavier than his dad, but Jim always said that Hoss missed the line where God was passing out brains. Hoss was a little slower thinking than most folks were and was made fun of in grade school until he was a head taller than the other kids were. He beat the crap out of the two bullies that had been abusing him, and no one ever picked on him again. Luckily, he was a kindhearted giant and was nice to everyone.

Jim heard the truck back out of the garage and knew he was right about the Solar Flare or EMP. He stepped back into the house and retrieved his Taurus 9mm pistol, holster, and extra magazines.

"Hoss we were attacked by some damn country with Electro Magnetic Pulse bombs. We would have heard about a Solar Flare way in advance of it striking the Earth. Drive! Take me to the crash."

"This is the Captain we just circled around Nashville and will be at cruising speed and altitude in about five minutes. The city of Lebanon will be below the right wing in a few seconds, and then we will cross the Cumberland River on our way to Charlotte. Please keep your seat.... Oh shit."

The lights went off, and no emergency lights came on as the passengers heard the engines wind down and die. The plane leveled off for a few seconds and started to descend. There was chaos, screaming, and praying throughout the cabin.

A stewardess ran down the aisle yelling, "Keep your seat belt buckled, lower your heads, and place your hands over your heads. We've lost power, and the pilot is going to find a place to land.

The Captain looked over at the Copilot and said, "Everything is dead. We can't make it back to Nashville, but can we double back and land at Lebanon?"

"No, we're dropping too fast. We will be down before we can turn around and line up with the runway. I know the land ahead. There are plenty of farms ahead that we can use to belly land."

"I hate it, but I think you are right. Prepare to land."

"I'm looking for an open field without trees. Damn, we're down to 500 feet. Now 250. Here we go 100 feet. Try to get the nose up!"

The jet touched down then bounced ten feet in the air before skidding through the cornfield tearing fences down and leaving a wide swath of downed corn seedlings.

"Damn, we're going to hit that bridge over the creek ahead. Brace for impact."

The plane hit the small concrete bridge and tore apart. The cockpit exploded upon impact, and the rest of the aircraft cartwheeled to the left breaking the wings of and the cabin into three sections. The wings and the front part of the fuselage burst into flames while the rear part fell into the shallow creek.

Bob stayed up all night worried about his family in Louisville and was not surprised when the lights flickered and died. He checked his Samsung Galaxy phone and radio and as he suspected they were all dead. He went to his garage and opened a galvanized steel garbage can and fished out several 50 Caliber ammo boxes and took an emergency radio and a pair of walkie-talkie out of the boxes, and then stored the boxes back in his makeshift Faraday Cage.

Before he turned the radio on it dawned on him to look for plane crashes. He had studied EMPs in the Army and knew what to expect so he took his binoculars out to the deck and surveyed the area towards Nashville as he hoped not to see anything bad.

"Crap, there are several columns of black smoke toward Nashville," he said to himself."

He watched for a few minutes and caught a glimpse of a plane flying low heading right at him. He watched it come down west of him about a couple of miles.

"Damn, it might have crashed into the river. I need to go help."

He went into the house, strapped on his .45 Ruger pistol, grabbed his 12 Gauge pump and his Bugout Bag, and headed to the garage. Bob ran past his 2023 F350 and jumped into his '50 FI Ford 4x4 that he had built himself. He stored his gear and turned the key to the old truck. It fired right up, and he raced north toward Dixon Springs so he could drive east to Hartsville to get across the river and head down South to the crash. He was only two miles from the accident as the Crow flies but over twenty miles away since there were only two bridges across the river in his area.

He was on Rome Road driving about 60 MPH when he saw a man up ahead trying to flag him down. He recognized the man and slowed down then stopped beside his friend.

"Bob, what happened?"

"I don't have time to talk. We were attacked by an EMP bomb. A plane crashed on the east side of the river, and I'm going to see if I can help the poor souls."

"I'll go with you."

54

Greg Farmer was a local man who had sold part of his farm to Bob. They became friends and swapped stories about their days in the Army. Greg was a little younger than Bob, and his wife was a couple of years younger than Greg was. Greg's daughter and her two girls lived with him and helped around his farm and store in Dixon Springs. Greg owned the local Ace Hardware Store.

Bob said, "Greg, I see you have a Glock strapped to your hip. You know your store will be looted in about two days when people realize what happened."

"Yes, that's one of the reasons I flagged you down. I would like you to stop on the way in so I can tell Wilma to close the store and then stop again on the way back home and let me gather a few supplies, guns, and ammo from my store."

"Not a problem but hurry."

"Thanks, how long before the power is back on?"

"My guess is that it will take years for the major cities. Five to ten years for smaller cities and perhaps not in our lifetime for a rural area like we live in."

"Boy, I hope you are wrong. Why so long?"

"You've seen those big transformers sitting on the side of the road with a bunch of smaller transformers around them that send power out to small villages and subdivisions."

"Yes, why?"

"Most of all transformers were fried by the EMP. The small ones and the ones at our houses are manufactured in the USA. The large ones are only made in South Korea and China. There is very few held in reserve since they are very expensive to make. It will take years to set up manufacturing capability and then more years to install the large and small ones."

"Oh shit."

"Yep, we are up shit creek without a paddle. Fucked and far from home. Shit out of luck...."

"I get it, Bob. What's next?"

"People die from starvation, lack of medicine and medical care, and murder. There will be riots and looting when the food runs out, and then my favorite, the unfed hordes of Walking Democrats will leave the large cities looking for food, drugs, guns and women."

"Hey, I'm a Democrat. We are just as civilized as any damned Republican."

"Greg, I'm mainly talking about the ones that have been fed, sheltered and had free everything for the most of their lives. They will be the first wave. The second wave will be ordinary people who will kill good God fearing people to steal a loaf of bread to feed their kids."

"You paint a horrible picture."

"And I was holding back some of the bad stuff. I've been studying this crap for many years. My son thinks I'm nuts. Be happy that your daughter and grandkids are with you. Mine are somewhere on the highway heading this way."

They entered Dixon Springs and drove up to Greg's hardware store. Wilma was sitting in a chair talking with one of the locals.

"Greg, I didn't open the store. No need to without power."

Bob poked Greg and said, "They'll probably get the power back on after they get the lines back up."

"Wilma, go on home. I'll check back in a couple of hours and decide to open or not. Please post a note saying the store is closed."

Bob, "Why didn't you want them to know what happened?"

"Because it gives us time to go to the crash and get back before they are all frantic. Let's move the plane went down 30 minutes ago."

They saw numerous cars, and tractor-trailers stopped along the main road out of Dixon Springs and passed several people wanting rides. Bob flew past them and said, "Remember those Kroger and Walmart trucks. We may want to come back and see if they have anything we need."

"That's stealing. You can't just take what you want."

"Those trucks are abandoned and will be looted within three to five days."

They took back roads to go below Hartsville to avoid the city and crossed the bridge at Highway 141. They only traveled a few miles south before they saw the smoke from the crash. Bob speeded up and was soon on the road in front of the crash. There were a truck and several people at the site of the accident. Bob drove through the corn to where the other truck was, and they went to join the others.

"Are there any left alive, and how can we help?"

A big man stepped up and said, "We have checked the wreckage over there and will check that part of the fuselage to the left. Please check the tail section in the creek."

"Will do," Bob said as they ran over to the tail section.

"Bob I hear voices," Greg said, as they got closer to the wreck.

"Help. Help us."

The tail section had settled at the bottom of the shallow creek bed, and the open end was blocking the flow of water. The water had backed up and was now four feet deep in the cabin.

Bob waded into the cabin along with Greg and started helping the victims get out to the creek bank. There were 23 people in the cabin, but only five were still alive.

They helped the women first and then came back for the three men. They carried the women but could only drag the men out of the watery grave. Several had broken arms or legs but thank God, there were no gaping wounds to deal with. Bob didn't realize until later that those people had bled to death.

"Greg, make them comfortable until we can figure out how to get them to a hospital."

Bob walked over to the big man and noticed the pickup was gone.

"Hey, I'm Bob Karr, and I live just a short piece across the river. We saw the crash and got here as fast as we could."

"Glad to meet ya'. I'm Jim Dickerson, and I live a few miles east of here. I saw you dragging out some survivors, so I sent my son back to the farm to bring a trailer to help take these poor people to the hospital."

"Thanks. There are only five survivors out of 23 in the tail section."

"Everyone else is dead. You know that we've been attacked don't you."

"Bob replied, "Yeah, some sort of nuclear EMP. We have bad times ahead."

"Yes and I noticed both of you had shootin' irons on your hips. That's a good thing."

Greg and Bob stayed to help load the survivors onto the trailer and then left to go back to Greg's store. Jim Dickerson took the injured to the hospital in Lebanon.

They pulled back into Dixon Springs an hour later and found a crowd of people in front of the Quick Pick gas station across the street from Greg's store. Bob pulled around the store to the back entrance, and Bob walked over to the crowd to see what was going on while Greg loaded what he came to get into the truck.

One man in the crowd was very loud, and Bob heard him say, "I'm telling you that something bad has happened and we need to prepare for the worst."

A woman said, "Don't get crazy. The Government will be here soon to help. The power will be back on by tonight, and this will blow over."

Bob yelled, "Listen up! Now that I have your attention. Do any of your phones work?"

Everyone replied, no.

"Do any of your cars or trucks run?"

Another round of no's was heard.

One man asked, "Why is yours running?"

"I'll get to that in a minute. Do any of your TVs, radios or other electronics work?"

Again nothing but no was heard."

"Okay, my truck runs because it doesn't have any electronic parts on it. If you have vehicles manufactured before about 1974, they should run also. Old tractors, pickups, and such will run."

"Why will they run?"

"Because we have been attacked with nuclear EMP bombs and that fried all electronics that weren't shielded by a metal cage. The power won't be coming back on for a long time. We need to band together and help each other survive this nightmare."

"Why do you know so much about this?"

"It was part of my job and training in the military. That's why I bought the old truck and have been getting ready for this for several years."

"What do we need to do?"

"First thing is to only eat refrigerated or frozen foods first. You won't have a working refrigerator so eat that stuff first. Second, boil or put a small amount of bleach in your drinking water. We need to have a meeting to cover the rest later today. Let's meet at the shelter in the park at say 2:00 pm."

"Hey, I'm from Riddleton. We need to invite them also."

"My advice is that Riddleton is okay to invite but don't expand beyond that. You don't want strangers taking over your meeting and lives."

"You have the only truck running. Can you come over and pick us up?"

"No. I only have so much gas, and the pumps aren't working. Ride a bicycle or walk."

"Well, that's not neighborly."

"Get used to solving your own problems. There are fifty old cars and trucks behind barns in this area. Get them running. Hell, some of you have antique tractors, cars, and trucks. Use them for transportation. Pick your neighbor up and share the ride. Take gas from the new vehicles that won't run and fill the old car's tanks."

Bob saw Greg wave at him, so he backed out of the crowd and walked over to him, and they drove on back to Greg's home and unloaded the supplies.

"Bob, take half of the ammo and get some of the camping and survival gear. I can't use it all."

"Thanks, Greg. Does your old GMC run?"

"Yes, if it had a battery and some tires."

"Take the battery from your daughter's car and put it in the truck. I'll keep an eye out for older GM wheels with tires."

Jim and Hoss drove down to State Road 24 East and headed into Lebanon. The Hospital was only about 16 miles from the crash site, but their progress was slow because of all of the crashed and stalled cars. Several people tried to stop them and ask for a ride, but Jim kept driving, and Hoss warned them to get away.

They drove up to several crashed vehicles that blocked the road and saw several people laid out on the ground with their heads covered. Then they saw a man waving at them to stop. There were a young woman and a child with blood smeared all over them. Jim stopped and helped them into the wagon.

"We're taking these people to the hospital and you look like you need a hospital so let's help you onto the wagon."

"Thanks, Mister. I don't know what's going on, but I didn't see an ambulance or the police."

"I think they are busy. This looks like it may have hit the entire state or even the country."

"God, I hope not."

They arrived at the hospital, and Jim drove up to the emergency entrance. To his surprise, no one came out to help get the injured people into the emergency room. People were milling around the entrance and several people lying on the ground.

Jim and Hoss each carried one of the women into the emergency room where a nurse yelled, "Get them out of here. We will triage them to see who has the most severe injuries."

"I have five from a plane crash and two from a car wreck."

"Sir we have hundreds of injured people. Park them by the door, and I'll be out to check on them in a few minutes."

They helped the people to the triage area, and then they drove away hoping to get back home quickly. They only got to the center of town when two Deputy Sheriffs stopped them.

"Sheriff Johnson told us to stop any vehicles and requisition them for official use. Please get out and give us your keys."

"Over my dead body. Tell Buck to get his sorry ass out here and try to take my truck himself," Jim said as he raised the Taurus so the officers could see it pointed at them.

One of the Deputies ran into the Wilson County Sheriff Department building and came back walking beside Buck Johnson the Wilson County Sheriff.

"Now Jim why you giving Floyd a rash of shit? This is an emergency, and I need that truck."

"Wish in one hand and shit in the other and see which one fills up the fastest. You ain't taking this truck."

Hoss pointed the business end of a 12 Gauge pump at the Sheriff and grunted.

"Well I guess you have the drop on us this time, but I'll remember this the next time I see you, boys."

"You'd better remember not to try to steal from your citizens, or you won't be Sheriff much longer."

A tall, thin man walked up behind the Sheriff and said, "Buck, what are you and Jim arguing about?"

"The pot-bellied excuse of a Sheriff is trying to confiscate my truck."

"Buck, that's not called for yet. You should have politely asked Jim to help you with transportation until we get some vehicles running."

"Bye Senator O'Berg. I'm going home and see if my neighbors need help," Jim said as he drove off.

The Senator and Sheriff went back into the Sheriff's meeting room and rejoined the discussion in progress.

"Barry, we need to declare martial law and get ahead of this before we have riots and looting."

"I agree. Buck, you need to deputize about 25 more of our good citizens to help keep the peace. Jerry, you need to get the city garage looking for older vehicles that don't have electronic ignition and get them running. We need police cars, ambulances and dump trucks to haul away the trash."

"I'll get right on it Senator."

"Now Senator O'Berg, I'm the Mayor of Lebanon, and I should give the direction and orders to my department heads."

"That would normally be correct; however, this is a national disaster, and as the highest ranking Federal Official I am taking charge of the recovery effort."

The Mayor shut up and sat down.

"Now, Tom, close all stores, food warehouses, and restaurants until we can get an inventory of what food is available.

Buck, have your men begin confiscating all semi-automatic pistols and rifles. For public safety, only hunting rifles and shotguns will be allowed to be in private hands in Wilson County. No one except County and City Officials will be allowed in town with firearms."

The Mayor spoke up, "Some of our citizens won't like these orders. We don't have the authority to take these actions."

"The Senator looked around the room and asked, "How many of you agree with the Mayor? Raise your hands."

"No one raised their hand."

"Mayor Jacobs. You are officially removed from office, and you must clear your personal possessions and go home."

"You can't do this."

"I just did. Go!"

"Paul, round up the ranchers and farmers and tell them that there will be a food shortage in a few weeks and we need them to step up production to feed this area. They must designate all of their food production to Wilson County until we have a surplus and can trade it for other things we need to survive."

The men around the Senator would normally be balking at this power grab and Federal intrusion on their County, but they had just seen their electricity go off, cars and electronic devices fail, and planes fall from the sky. They were scared, this man knew what to do in this crisis, and they fell in lock step with him.

Senator Barry O'Berg was only a second term Democratic Senator who had moved to Lebanon eight years ago, but he had money and backing from the major money men in the Democratic party. He had already started his campaign for President, and most of the liberal media loved him. No one cared that he had ties to the Mob families in Chicago and New York or that his mentor was a radical terrorist from the '60s. He was truly a Teflon candidate. He promised free health care, free health care, no taxes for anyone but the wealthy, and a reduction in military spending.

"Joan what the fuck is going on. Have you contacted my staff in DC or anyone in the military to see what happened?"

"Senator, there are no communications with anyone. Your wife is driving the locals nuts with her demands to get back to DC."

64

"Well if we're stuck here, I'll just make the best of it. Tell Chris to join me in my office. Give my wife a bottle of vodka and some pills."

The Senator's 27-year-old blonde trophy wife was as dumb as she was beautiful. He left his wife years ago for her when she was only 21 and a low-level clerk in his office. His wife caught them at a motel and threw him out. His daughter never forgave him, and she would not visit with him.

The Senator cursed the world, the blackout, and the Russians because he knew they had to be behind this mess."

"Chris, get one of those old trucks and drive to Nashville and see if you can get us a flight back to DC. Try the Military if you have to.

"Buck, send a couple of your Deputies up into Kentucky and see if you can find Maddie. She was on a field trip going to Mammoth Cave when the lights went out. I'm beside myself thinking the worse," said the Senator.

"Now Barry, you know my men don't...."

"Do you want to keep your job?"

"Well, yes sir."

"Then get your fat ass in gear and find my wayward daughter. My Chief of Security would make a fine Sheriff don't you think?"

"No need of that. We'll find a car that runs and fetch her down here in a New York minute."

Bob left and headed toward home when he remembered those Kroger and Walmart trucks dead on the highway. He drove home, hitched up his cargo trailer, and headed back to the vehicles taking care to drive around town. He also took a different route by Greg's house so Greg wouldn't see the trailer.

The trucks were still there, and the drivers had left their loads. Most of the people stranded on the road were walking home or to their destination. There were only one or two walking by every now and then.

He stopped behind a Walmart truck and backed his trailer up to the end of the semi-trailer. He cut the lock with bolt cutters and saw that the two end pallets were canned goods for the grocery department. He dropped box after box from the trailer down to the back of his trailer with many falling to the ground. He got down and started stacking the boxes in the front of his trailer.

He was smiling ear to ear because he had hit pay dirt. The boxes contained everything from canned meat to pork and beans.

He was busy stacking boxes when he heard, "Walmart won't like you stealing their groceries."

He thought quickly and said, "I work for Walmart, and they sent me here to get as much as possible on this trailer and take it to the store in Lebanon. The bastards could have sent me some help. I'll pay you with food if you help me load my trailer."

"Mister I just live a mile from here, and my son I will help you load this up if you will drop my son and me at my house with a small part of this food."

"Deal."

They worked for several hours until the trailer and pickup bed were full of boxes. Bob drove to the man's house and helped him, and his son unload twenty boxes of food."

"Thanks, sir. Food will be scarce in a couple of days."

"I'm glad that you could help. Could you give me a hand again this evening? I'll drop this trailer off and bring another."

"I'd be glad too, but won't Walmart miss the food you gave me."

"Son, what we don't take will be looted in two days."

"Then I'll go back with my wheelbarrow and get some of the Kroger food."

"Have at it."

"Mister, if the Lebanon Walmart needed the groceries why is the truck headed away from Lebanon?"

"That's above my pay grade. I just lump boxes when they tell me to."

"Most box handlers don't have a pistol on their hip and an assault rifle in the cab of their antique pickup."

"You got me there. I'll pick you up about 4:00 pm."

"Okay. Hey, I'm Jack Fulkerson, and this is my son Tony. He and his family live next to us."

"I'm Bob. Please, ta' meet ya. Hey, we're having a meeting at the shelter to discuss the situation at 2:00. Why don't you and Tony join us."

Bob looked at his watch and saw that it was 12:15 and thanked God he had one of the few windup watches left in the modern world. He had to be back in town for the meeting at 2:00 so he dropped the trailer in the barn, cleaned up, and ate some cold hotdogs and a beer for lunch. Then he drove back toward town and picked up Greg along the way into town. He parked in the parking lot to the shelter. He and Greg were amazed at the creativity in the types of vehicles parked in front of the shelter. There were bicycles, old cars, trucks, riding lawn mowers, and several horses.

The folks were milling around, and it was evident that no one was leading the group.

"Greg, you know these people. I think you should take charge until they figure out how to elect a leader."

"I don't want to, but I think you are right," he said and then raised his voice to say, "The meeting will come to order. I'm taking charge until you elect someone so we can get this show on the road."

They all sat down on the picnic tables and lawn chairs to listen to Greg. None complained about him taking leadership. Hell, they just wanted someone to tell them what to do.

"Bob will start by telling us what happened."

Bob stood up and explained why their power, cars, and electronics failed, and then added, "I don't know who or why we were nuked, but that is what happened.

Now we all need to band together to help keep our area secured and our families fed while we try to regroup from this disaster. There are a lot of things that have to happen during the next two days that will shape if we survive or die."

There were talking and arguing throughout the group until Bob rapped the butt of his .45 on a table.

"I know that I am painting a pretty dire picture; however, this is a dire situation. We need to find clean drinking water, food, guns, and ammo to survive. I'll go into more detail later, but you have to accept that we will work hard to get those items and someone else will try to take them away from us to feed their own families.

Criminals, thugs, and God fearing people will kill you for a can of beans in two to four weeks. You must be ready to fight to keep what you have and to get what you need to survive. We need to put someone in charge of each of these vital duties."

All but a few of the people started to wander off and made comments that Bob was full of crap and the government would come to take care of them.

Bob surprised the thirty some odd people that remained seated in the shelter by saying, "Good riddance to people that will either rob you or kill you later this month. Those folks will be just as dangerous as any criminal from the city that comes to rob you."

Greg replied, "Most of them are good people. I think you are judging them too harshly."

"I saw a few hard working people in the bunch, but I also saw a double hand full of Meth addicts, drug pushers, and lifetime welfare cheats. The people sitting here are mostly farmers, store owners or employed hard working people. Almost all of you live down in the bend where I live. We are protected by the river on three sides and can defend our people, food, and possessions.

The shit hit the fan today. The Grid is down. In three days, the stores will be empty, a few days later the warehouses and trucks stalled on the roads will be looted. These people will be starving and come to your farms to take your food and your crops."

All of the people were shaking their heads in agreement, one stood up and asked, "What do we do to prepare?"

"First there are three trucks full of food out on the highway that we need to go get and store in a safe place. I need half of you to go with me in your trucks to bring it back here. Second, Greg, you and Harold need to empty your stores of everything we need to survive and take it back to your homes or one of our barns. Third, Ned, bring several of those 500-gallon water tanks and some hand pumps to Harold's gas station and fill everyone's cars and trucks, and then fill the tanks and store them in a safe place. Fourth, always be armed and ready to defend yourselves. Fifth, I will work on training our security force and improve our overall security. Sixth, we need to elect a leader, a sheriff and find people with medical skills. And last, we'll need to find a way to help pay Harold and Greg for what we use from their stores.

That's enough to get started."

"Bob, what if outsiders or those people come with guns to take our food?"

Bob patted his .45 and said, "We are not going to let that happen. We will out think, out shoot and out survive any of those slackers."

*

Chapter 4

Day One – Complications

Shorty was right about them drawing attention as they ran down the middle of Highway 65 South. They both had their running clothes on and stood out among the people stranded on the highway. Jo suggested that they put T-shirts over their running gear to hide the pistols, so they stopped and put them on to blend in a bit better.

They stopped a couple of times to answer questions but quickly learned to keep running and ignore the stranded motorists. They talked some along the way, but Jo was focused on getting to her kids and mother as fast as possible.

Her chest hurt like hell and every time she took a deep breath, it hurt worse. Both had a backpack with 25 pounds of gear and Bill was pushing the Ironman Jogging Stroller. She mentioned the pain to her husband, and he gave her a pain pill and a big gulp of water. That helped, and her mind was soon off the pain in her chest and back to worrying about the kids and her Mom.

They had been running for four hours, and she felt better as the miles melted away. Her feet felt great, and she loved her Altra 4.0 Provision running shoes. They were expensive but well worth the extra dough. She had a pair of hiking boots in the stroller, but couldn't run a mile in them without killing her feet.

"Bill, did you tape your nips?"

"You know I did. That hurts like hell when I run long distance if I don't tape them. You didn't forget did you with those big ones of yours?"

"Hell yes. We were in a hurry, and now my nipples are starting to chafe."

"I've got a pack of Nipease. Let's pull off in the bushes up ahead, and I'll stick some on your tits."

"You haven't paid much attention to my tits in a while. Why the interest now?"

"I just wanted to be helpful. I've always liked your perky tits. I don't want them rubbed raw."

They stopped behind the bushes, and she pulled her shirt up exposing her breasts to her husband who applied one of the clear bandages to each nipple before gently squeezing the right one.

"The right one was always your favorite. Sorry, that's all you get today, and I'll be too damned bushed to fool around tonight."

They were still fresh and making about four miles an hour so, they decided to only take a quick rest at 24 miles and trudge on to the north side of Elizabethtown the first day. Jo calculated, in her mind, that they would stop at about 9:00 pm and set up camp for the night.

She took over pushing the stroller at 20 miles and pushed it until they stopped. She had pushed all of her kids in strollers like this, but it had been years since Jake was small enough to push around in a stroller. It seemed much harder now than it did back then, but of course, she was getting older. She hated the getting older part of life.

"Bill I think we can keep running until we run out of gas. It will be dark without the moon. Let's see if we can get through Glasgow instead of stopping before the town."

"Okay if you let me push the stroller after we hit E-town."

They laughed and joked about running for their lives, pushing a stroller across the USA and a hundred other things as they chatted while jogging into E- Town. She found herself enjoying her husband's company for the first time in a year. He had been very distant since he got jealous of her partner Walt. Bill didn't know about Walt hitting on her, but somehow sensed Walt's interest. He asked her to get another partner, and when she balked, he sulked for a while then acted as if he didn't care.

"Look up ahead there are several buildings on fire."

"Bill, they're probably from a combination of airplane crashes and looting. You might have to use that gun you hate if someone tries to rob or kill us."

"I won't kill anyone for taking stuff. I would never let someone harm you or the kids and would do my best not to harm them if I could."

Bill pushed the stroller, and they jogged on into E-Town until they saw Highway 210, which was the road to Glasgow. There wasn't an exit, so Bill lifted the stroller over the concrete barrier and they carefully walked down the embankment to the road below and then headed south. They didn't know it, but they were following the same route their kids and Jo's Mom had taken that day.

They had just merged onto Hodgenville Road when a woman came running out of a subdivision on their left yelling and waving at them.

"Help! My daughter has been shot!"

Jo replied, "Mam you need to find a Doctor."

Bill asked, "Where is she?"

"A block and a half that way," she pointed as she replied.

"Come on Jo. I need to help her."

Jo looked disgusted but replied, "Who shot her and is he still in the area."

'It's her boyfriend, and yes, he is in the house across the street robbing his dad."

They followed the woman to her house, and Jo made sure it was safe for Bill to enter before heading to the house across the street.

Jo drew the Glock and cautiously walked up to the house. She peered into a bedroom window and saw a man tied up and gagged. He had a large hole in his head, and blood was everywhere. She went on to the living room window and carefully looked around the edge of the window. There was a young man with a gun trained on a woman and her young son. They were stuffing cash and other valuables into a pillowcase.

Jo couldn't shoot through the window for fear of the robber shooting his hostages or her bullet striking one of them. She thought that if she waited for him to leave that she could get a clear shot at him away from the hostages. She hid in the bushes for ten minutes and wondered why he hadn't left. She snuck back to the window and saw the bastard was sitting on the couch

74

eating a sandwich, and his hostages were bound and gagged on the floor.

She noticed his pistol was beside his drink and decided to take a shot. She edged around to get her Glock in position, and the man reached for his pistol and stood up facing her. Jo shot, first, and glass exploded on her, as the bullet hit the man in the stomach. The man got off a wild shot that missed Jo. Jo shot again and hit the man in the center of his chest knocking him back down to the couch.

Jo ran into the house and took the gun from the dead man's hand. She checked his pulse and confirmed what her common sense told her. A shot near the heart and a shot to the stomach are not good for the human body. The scumbag was dead. Jo ran over to the woman, who was screaming and untied her.

The woman almost knocked Jo down running to the robber. She grabbed him in her arms and cried, "My boy is dead. You bitch. You shot my son."

The woman tried to hit Jo, but Jo restrained her and tried to remind her that her son had killed her husband, shot a woman next door, and robbed her. The woman wouldn't listen but finally calmed down enough so that Jo could untie her young son.

Jo looked at the teenaged boy and said, "Take care of your mom. It will be a few days before she gets her head straight. Where did you get the black eye and bruises?"

"Mom hits me. Thanks for saving our lives. Matt was going to kill Mom and me before he left. He hated all of us, and Mom just pampered him and fed his drug problem."

"Son, if that's the truth, then you need to get away from her. Are there any families that will take you in around here?"

"Yes, I'm going to my best friend's house about a mile from here. I can't help Mom. She's on Oxy, and when that is gone, she'll be dangerous."

"Pack a bag and go now before she tries to harm you again. I'll arrest her and get her to a hospital for treatment."

The boy packed and was soon on his way. Jo walked back into the living room, picked up the thug's gun, and shot the woman in the back of the head.

"Bitch you won't hurt any kids anymore."

Jo ran to the bathroom and puked into the toilet. She had never shot at a man before yesterday and now had killed three people. She walked over to the home next door and found Bill working on the young girl.

"Jo, thank God you are okay. We heard the gunshots, and I was scared to death. What happened?"

The man who shot this poor girl killed his father and mother. He was going to kill his brother, but I arrived in time to stop him. Everyone but the brother is dead. The boy is going to stay with his best friend's family. How is this girl?"

"She was shot trying to keep the man from shooting her mom. It's a through and through wound to her left bicep. I cleaned her up and gave her a bottle of antibiotics. She should be fine in a couple of weeks."

"That's good. I'm going back to see about getting those folks buried. I'll be back in a few minutes."

Jo stepped outside and saw a crowd gathered around the house. She pulled her badge out and waved it at the crowd.

"Does anyone know this family?"

"Several people responded with yes."

"The drugged out son shot a girl across the street, his own dad, and mom before I shot him."

"That sounds like the worthless piece of shit," a man in the crowd stated.

"I don't think any police are going to show up to handle this. You need to bury the three of them in their back yard."

"What do you mean the police won't show up? Why not?"

"People, the grid is down, your phones don't work, and your town is starting to burn down. There is rampant looting, and half of E-Town will be charred ruins in three days. Look over toward the city. You are on your own."

The crowd looked west and saw a dozen black plumes of smoke rising above the city. They started arguing among themselves and then most went back to their houses.

One lady said, "You are a cop. Protect us."

"I was a cop in Louisville. I quit and am looking out for myself. Bury them or burn the house down around them. I don't have to live with the stink from the bodies," Jo said as she walked back to the other house.

"Bill, are you ready to leave?"

"Darling someone needs to watch over this poor girl."

"Bill, we will see dozens of girls like this in the next few days. We can't keep stopping and risk being killed ourselves. That asshole got a lucky shot off, and only God and a brick wall saved my ass this time. Come with me or stay. Bye."

Jo gathered her backpack, rifle from the baby stroller and a handful of the water bottles and walked towards the main road. A few minutes later Bill ran up beside her pushing the stroller and waved for her to stop.

"Jo please put the rifle and water bottles back into the stroller. I'm with you. I love you, but it's hard walking away from injured people. I am trained to save lives not let them die."

"Bill I'm also trained to save lives; but I'm trying to save our family's and our own lives. We have to ignore everyone else and keep focused on our family. Your Dad had told you for years that when the shit hits the fan, millions will die. In three months, over 200 million Americans will be dead. We have a head start on them thanks to your Dad, and I don't want to squander that advantage helping everyone on the way just to find my kids and Mom dead."

Jo, surely you don't believe this crap. I'm only going along with this trip to help make sure you and the kids get there safely. The Government will clear this up and have the power back on before the end of the week."

"Bill that is a joke. The Government won't do shit besides rounding people up and putting them in FEMA camps. You are a wimp. You will not protect yourself, much less the kids or me. I'm tired of your liberal shit, and you can go where ever the hell you want to, but don't slow me down again or I'll leave your sorry ass."

She took off running and left him behind. It was fifteen minutes before he caught up to her. He ran beside her and kept his mouth shut. She remembered back several years as she ran beside the man she once loved with all her heart. They had disagreements on politics but never got angry until Bill got jealous. She wanted her old Bill back that was kind, considerate, and funny.

"Bill, pull over for a few minutes."

"Okay."

"Bill, I know that you are jealous of Walt. Yes, the bastard made a pass at me, but I set him straight and planned to get another partner next week. Nothing ever happened between us. I swear to God. Bill, I want my old Bill back. The one that is a kind and gentle father and a great lover. I don't like this mean jealous streak in you."

78

"I'm only jealous because you chose him over me."

"I didn't choose him over you. It would have been my word against his. It would have been an ugly situation. I applied for a transfer to the precinct in our neighborhood and would have been transferred in a couple of weeks."

"So he was harassing you."

"Yes, but just the innuendo and pet names. He liked to call me doll. I liked Walt at first until he got this crush on me. Without evidence against him, he would have gotten mad and spread vicious lies about me to the men at the station. That would hurt my career and kill promotions. It's hard for a woman to advance in the police force without sleeping her way to the top."

"Why didn't you tell me this? I love you and would have understood."

"And your pride would have made you confront the asshole, and he would have beaten the crap out of you or killed you. You're not a fighter. Walt is a highly trained military, and police trained professional."

"But I would have died like a man," Bill replied.

"Now I know you are pulling my leg my pacifist husband."

That was Bill's ah ha and oh shit moment all rolled into one. He thought about how his wife viewed him and decided that minute to make a change in his life.

Bill reached out to Jo and pulled her close to him. He kissed her gently and held onto her for a few minutes.

"Darling I love you and never want to lose you. Let's go find our kids," he said as he pushed the stroller back onto the road.

They ran in silence for a while before Jo broke the ice, "Darling we lost two hours back there, but the good news is we weren't running during that time and are somewhat rested. It's a

79

little after 5:00 now, and I think I can make it another four hours. Can you?"

"Yes and that gives us a good night's sleep. We can be on the road again at daybreak. My guess is we will stop about five miles below Hodgenville. That's not as far as we planned but still not bad for pushing a stroller and stopping to help those people."

"I'm sorry for blasting you about stopping to help that girl. I'm worried that our kids may be attacked on the way down. They started early in a car, so I'm hoping they were more than halfway there before the lights went out."

"I understand. Thanks to Dad, Will has learned a lot about survival and living off the land. He will be a big help to Jane getting them down to Dad's place. I know I should have listened to my Dad more about the outdoors stuff, but I was too busy running track and chasing girls."

"Yes you should have, but I ran track also, and that's how we met, and I was the girl you chased. I can't argue too much on that topic."

"It's a strange turn of events when two long distance runners have to run for their lives during an apocalypse. It would make a great book or perhaps an Amazon movie."

"I think Natalie Portman would play me, and Ben Affleck would play you in the movie."

"Matt Damon and Selma Hayek are a better fit. Hayek has big boobs like you."

"Ah after a year of not paying attention to me or my boobs, you are fixated on them."

"I always loved your boobs and the way they jiggle when you run."

"Enough boob talk for tonight. Save that for a couple of days, and we will explore the topic thoroughly."

"Promise?"

"Yes, I promise."

"Look up ahead," Jo, exclaimed.

They had just left Hodgenville, and the sun was now setting in the west. There was a crowd of people heading their way. The group stood out because they had flashlights with the beams dancing all around them. They were about half a mile up ahead and had not spotted Jo or Bill yet.

"Let's duck out of sight until they pass. I don't want any trouble with a crowd that large."

"Hon they are just poor stranded people on their way home."

"Bill, trust me. Get off the road now," Jo said as she pulled off in the bushes with Bill lagging behind but finally following her.

They watched as the group came closer to their hiding spot. There were six or more men in orange jumpsuits armed with a few rifles and clubs. They had obviously escaped from jail or prison and were walking to the closest town. To Jo's horror, she saw two young women and a teenage boy walking with the convicts with their hands tied.

The men were only a few yards away when they heard their conversation.

"That's three cops that won't screw with us anymore."

"Anyone figure out why the bus died. A lot of cars are dead."

"Nope, I think God did it to let us free," one man said as he laughed.

Jo and Bill were listening to the conversation and Jo didn't see the snake crawling beside her foot. Bill looked over at his wife and saw the Copperhead. He reacted and struck the snake with the butt of his carbine. Jo snapped her head around and saw the dying snake. Bill had struck it just behind the head crushing the snake. Jo pushed it away and blew a kiss at Bill.

One of the men stood up and said, "I've got business to attend to," as he walked straight into the bushes beside Jo. She couldn't move fast enough to get out of view, so she grabbed the man and put a chokehold on him. He tried to throw her off, but Bill hit him on the head with his pistol and he collapsed.

"Hey Al, what the fuck are you doing?

There was no response, and another man yelled, "Go check on Al."

Jo picked the snake up and pushed its fangs into the man's ankle, and then quickly gathered her rifle and pack to join Bill several yards away.

"Great thinking on placing the snake on him," Bill whispered in Jo's ear."

"Thanks for saving me from the snake. You are my hero." Replied Jo.

The man found Al dead on the ground with a Copperhead stuck to his ankle. He ran back to the group out of breath and said," Al got snake bit and died. The lucky bastard choked the snake to death before he died."

"Damn, that's a bad way to die."

"I don't give a shit about Al. I am just glad we are free, and we have this tail to share tonight. Hell, let's cut over to that farmhouse with the lights on. There might be more guns and women."

"That sounds like a winner. Let's go."

The men helped their hostages climb over the fence, and they started walking through a plowed field to get to the farmhouse.

"Bill, we have to stop these men. They are going to rape those women and probably kill them."

"I thought we weren't going to stop and help people."

"I'm a cop. I can't stand by and let this happen."

"Jo, I'm a Nurse. I can't stand by and let people die."

"Oh shit. I get it now. Please help me free those women and the boy."

"What can I do?"

"We need to hit them before they get to the house. I can get two maybe three before they know what's happening. I need you to get two more."

"You mean to shoot?"

"Yes, Bill. Pretend those men are going to kill the kids and me and pull the trigger. Or pretend they are going to kill your patients."

He remembered that he no longer wanted to be a wimp, but could he kill people was another question.

"Bill, are you in?"

"Yes."

"You know how to shoot. Just remember to let your breath out and squeeze the trigger. Aim for body shots. A 9mm round will do the work and knock them on their asses. Oh, aim about six inches high. That 9mm carbine's bullet will drop quickly, and we haven't checked the sights.

Follow me to that stand of trees halfway to the house before they look back," Jo said.

83

Jo and Bill dropped their backpacks and ran across the soft plowed ground to the trees.

"Take cover behind a tree and use it to steady your rifle. I'll take the front three. You take the back two. Don't shoot if the hostages are in the line of fire. Shoot when you hear me shoot. Don't stop until they are all down."

The men were 75 yards from the stand of trees when Jo took a bead on the man in front. She breathed deep, let it out, and squeezed the trigger with the ball of her finger. The rifle kicked, there was a flash, and the man fell down. She moved her sights to the next man and repeated the process to shoot the second man. She heard several shots from Bill's direction.

Bill aimed and fired the Keltek missing his first man. He quickly aimed and fired again knocking the man down. He fired a dozen more times hitting three of the men.

The hostages took off running toward the house, and one man shot at them. Bill shot that man, and Jo shot the last man standing.

"Bill, good job. Let's make sure they are all dead," Jo yelled as she ran towards the men.

One rose up to shoot, and Jo shot three times, on the run, and blew half his face off. She walked up to each man and found three alive. She dispatched them with a headshot to put them out of their misery.

She looked around and didn't see her husband anywhere, so she ran back to the stand of trees and found him puking and crying at the same time.

"Bill, are you okay. Are you wounded?"

"I'm okay. I'm sorry, but I am that wimp my Dad always said I was."

"No Bill. That took guts to stand up to those men and stop them from harming those people. You also saved me from that damned snake. Hell, I puked my guts up after killing that drugged out guy today. Killing a person is one of the worst things a person can do, but sometimes we have to do it to save lives."

She looked up and saw a man walking toward the dead men. She thought this was the farmer from the house; however, the cop in her urged caution.

"Sir, Police. Please drop the shotgun."

"Okay," the startled man replied as he laid the gun down.

Jo saw the man was dressed in jeans and a T-shirt and asked, "Sir, do you live here?"

"Yes, we heard the shooting, and then the women and a boy came to our door seeking shelter. I came over here to keep those assholes from attacking my family. Did you shoot all of them?"

"We heard them planning to attack your house and had to stop them. We waited until they were out in the open and ambushed them from that stand of trees."

"Do you know anything about the power outage?"

"No, but my guess is that the USA has been attacked with nuclear bombs."

"That's what I was afraid of myself. I saw a Science Fiction movie once, and the lights went out cell phones, and cars stopped working."

"Sir, we're going to head on south. Can you take care of those people?"

"Yes, but I insist that you stay the night. It looks like you've been walking for a while."

"We started this morning in Louisville and have a hundred miles to go. Are you sure you have enough room?"

"If you don't mind a blow-up mattress. The others have our extra beds."

"That would be great. I wasn't looking forward to sleeping on the ground."

"Have you had supper?"

The food was great, and they had a cold shower, but they didn't get to bed until 11:00 pm. At least they had an air mattress and privacy since they were placed in the woman's sewing room. Jo locked the door and wedged a chair against the door handle so they wouldn't have to pull guard duty through the night.

Jo took her clothes off in front of Bill and then snuggled up against him.

"I thought you said you'd be too tired to fool around."

"That was before my big strong man saved me from a snake and shot the bad guys."

*

Chapter 5

Day One – Bob Takes the Lead

Bob hitched his flatbed trailer up and threw a tarp in the back of the bed to cover the food. He then drove back to Jack's home being careful to skirt around town and the one large subdivision. Jack and his son joined Bob in the cab of the truck, and they made the short trip to the trucks with the food.

Bob made use of what little time he had to ask Jack what he thought about the meeting, and Jack replied he was thankful for the information.

"Bob, I know we don't have time now, but we need to discuss our long-term survival."

Several of the men from the meeting had already arrived and were hurriedly loading food into their trucks and trailers. Bob pulled up to the Kroger truck and backed the end of the trailer up to the right side of the Kroger trailer. One of the men tried to wave him off, but he continued to back to within a few feet of the trailer.

"Hey bud this is ours, and you need to get away."

"Aren't you one of the assholes who wouldn't join our group?"

"Yes, and I'm still not. I'm taking my share of the food."

"Who told this jerk about the food?"

One of the men who had joined the group replied, "I told him. He is my brother in law. We can't keep all of this food to ourselves."

"That was our intention. I found the food and told the group that I would share the food with our group not everyone."

"We can't let them starve."

"They will starve because they are too lazy to farm or work for food."

"Bob, gun," Jack yelled.

Bob pulled his .45 from his holster and turned just in time to see a blast and bullet whiz by his head coming from the asshole. Bob aimed, squeezed his trigger, and fired hitting the man squarely in the chest above his heart. The man fell where he stood.

"You murdered my brother in law!"

"He shot first, and he tried to kill Bob," yelled Jack.

"Your brother in law was a worthless drug dealer before the shit hit the fan and you are stupid for bringing him here. He probably was going the trade the food for drugs."

"What am I going to tell my sister?"

"Tell her that her scumbag husband tried to kill a man and the man killed him in self-defense. The truth is always best."

The men picked the body up and placed it in the bed of the guy's pickup. They helped him load enough food for his family and his sister's but no extra. The man drove off to bury the body and explain what happened to his sister.

Jack told Bob, "That man's wife isn't much better than the dead man. She was a drug user and part-time prostitute who plied her trade over in Carthage. I do feel sorry for Gary having to tell the assholes wife and kids their husband and father is dead."

"I hated killing him, but he left me no choice. Hell, I'd be dead if you hadn't warned me. I owe you my life. Thanks."

"I think I know how you can help me and pay off that debt. I want to join your community. I was in the Army and handled base security at several small Army bases. We'll talk after we deliver the food to the barn."

They finished loading their trailers and took the loads to Greg's barn to store. They made several trips until all three trailers were empty.

The rest of the teams had also completed their assignments. There were ten 500 gallon tanks filled with gas stored in Bob's old barn, all of the supplies from the Quick Pick and Greg's hardware store were stored in a barn across the way from Bob, and every man and woman in the work details were armed.

Greg's wife had made some sweet tea, and the group sat under a shade tree and held a meeting before leaving for the day. They all swapped stories about the car wrecks, plane crashes, and kids whining because the power was out, but Bob could see that they had a purpose and these people were coming together as a family would during a crisis.

Bob said, "I think most of you know Jack Fulkerson. He and his family are joining our group."

They all shook hands and welcomed Jack to the team.

Betty Lou, Greg's wife, asked, "Bob, what do we do now?"

Bob looked around the yard at the thirty some odd couples and a few single people and said, "We organize, plan, and succeed. We need to name a leader, a sheriff who's in charge of security, and make assignments that focus on getting us through the next six days. Then we need a plan for the next month and then one for the next year."

Greg spoke up, "Bob, several of us have been discussing this, and we think you should be the leader."

Jack added, "Bob before you say no, could you at least take the job for a month to get us through the worst part. My discussion with you today convinced me that you know what to do to help us survive."

"Let me say something first, and you may not want me as your leader. Today I had to shoot one of your neighbors because he tried to kill me. Be prepared for that to happen numerous times in the future. Jack saved my life by yelling and warning me. Whoever takes leadership will have to rule as a dictator for those thirty days on security, food, water, and people issues. People will be trying to kill us for our food, crops, drugs and eventually our women."

"Betty Lou laughed at the women comment."

"Betty, the law will breakdown in the next two days. Scumbags will sell or trade anything to get drugs, food, and alcohol. The old adage that sex sells will take on a new meaning."

Greg asked, "Bob help us with this. What would you be dictating?"

"Everybody pulls their weight and works. Every adult learns to shoot and protect the group. Everyone learns at least two new skills to help the group survive. A six-person jury will judge all violations, criminal acts, and any disagreements. You will pick the jury. Jack will be in charge of security during my 30 days leadership. He is an ex-military security specialist.

There is more to come but as you can see these are tasks and policies to ensure the group survives and thrives.

Any questions?"

There were only a few policy questions and then Bob said, "I want a show of hands. Those that want me to lead our group for the next 30 days raise your hands. The majority wins."

Every hand was raised, and it was unanimous. They wanted Bob to lead them through the crisis.

"Thanks for having confidence in me to lead this fine group. I need help for the next 30 days and all of you and your kids above 11 years old will get age appropriate assignments. Right now, I need Betty Lou to become our secretary, and her first assignment is to make a list of everyone's names and list all of their skills beside their name. Highlight any police or military service."

"I'll be glad to do both."

"Now, Greg, you need to start a perpetual inventory of all of the group's supplies, food, and gas stored at the community warehouses. Sue, you are now our superintendent of schools. Figure out how to get our kids an education. I think we should stress skills they can use in this new world without calculators, computers, and Xboxes."

"I'll be glad to. That will also help keep them out of trouble. All parents should give each child a list of chores to perform every day. They are going to be bored, and bored children are trouble."

"The meeting is over; however, I need Greg, Jack, and two volunteers to discuss shutting off access to our place in the Horseshoe. I know some like Jack live above the town, but we may be forced to have everyone come down here to live for safety when the hordes leave the cities. If I lived up there, I'd move down here now before being run out."

Jack said, "There are five families and four singles that live above the horseshoe. Where would we live? Bob, that was one of the things, that I wanted to discuss with you today. I agree and want to move down here."

"Well, I gave that some thought, and there are plenty of houses available. The old Jenkins place and the Tiller place have been empty for over a year. There are five nice log cabins, on the west bank, that are empty, and I doubt that Greg will rent them to any hunters or fishermen this year. I'm sure that the ones needing housing can work something out with Greg. We could also haul several trailers down here for people to live in until we figure things out."

The group disbanded, and Greg took the remaining members into the kitchen to have their meeting. Harold Hunter and Ned Kelly joined the meeting. Harold had worked in construction before he bought the store and Ned had been in the Military Police.

"What do you think about sealing off our little peninsula and making it an island? The river is 300 – 400 feet across, which gives us a buffer from a major attack, but we have half a mile of open land at the top. Any ideas?"

"Yes, I think it's a great idea. I thought about this on the ride over here. I recommend that we quickly string Barbwire across the top of the Horseshoe with roving guards and then as fast as possible construct a more permanent barrier. The old nuclear plant over toward Hartsville should have plenty of steel that can be used to make a barrier."

Ned added, "I think Jack hit the nail on the head. We need something now and make it better later. We also need to pool our horses to help with guard duty. I have four, and I know several members of our group have horses."

"Our biggest problem is communication. With all electronics down, we are screwed when it comes to spreading the word."

Bob walked out to his truck and returned with three walkie-talkies. He gave one each to Greg, Jack, and Betty Lou.

"I have one more in my truck and another four in a Faraday cage back at the house. They only reach five to ten miles, but that is more than enough for around here."

"I thought all electronics were destroyed by the EMP blast," said Greg.

"Any electronics stored in a metal box or metal garage without windows should be okay. The metal blocks the EMP waves. This also brings up a major point. Without us becoming lawless looters, we need to find sealed trailers, oversea shipping containers, and metal pole barns and search them for vehicles, radios and other electronics that might come in handy for survival.

A TV and a DVD player will help break the boredom one day. I have a small shipping container buried in my backyard that doubles as a storm shelter that I placed several electronic items and I park my Kawasaki Mule in just in case something like this happens.

Again, we don't want to steal; however, this is our survival, and most buildings and dead vehicles are abandoned or will be abandoned this week. We need to get to the stuff before someone else does."

"I sure don't want my husband in jail or shot for looting," Betty Lou added.

Greg quickly responded, "I second that motion.

Bob smiled and said, "So, where do we look for food, medical supplies, guns, ammo, and vehicles?"

Betty Lou went to her living room and came back with a phone book," I assume that I can remember how to use this antiquated form of the internet to look up businesses."

That brought a round of laughter, and Greg replied, "See, that's why I keep her around. Beauty and brains."

While Betty Lou looked up targets, the men made a list of warehouses from memory. There were the usual Walmart Kroger and Lowes stores on the list, and they also had industrial supply and car dealerships on their list.

"Where is the closest rail siding where we can find trains loaded with trailers and shipping containers," asked Jack?

"I like your thinking, but the closest one is a few miles south of Nashville. We would have to drive about 50 miles each way exposing ourselves to people and police who would want our vehicles. I seriously doubt if there are very many groups thinking this far ahead right now, and I think we need to wait on that rail yard until the herd thins itself out before attempting that trip," replied Bob.

"Damn, that would be a gold mine."

"Yes, but this early most of the major retailers, transportation hubs, and gun shops will have guards just itching to shoot looters. We need to concentrate on abandoned vehicles on the highways, stores, and gun shops that we can barter with or talk out of items we need."

"How do we talk someone out of guns or food?"

Bob offered, "We invite them and their supplies to move here to live safely."

"Damn good idea, but we must vet them to make sure that we're not bringing another Hitler into our little community."

94

Betty Lou scratched her head and asked, "How do we start this search?"

Bob replied, "We need two small teams hitting our targets every day until we either bring home supplies from the target or mark it off our list. No team is to try to steal or force someone to give us anything. We are a week ahead of any other groups in our planning stage. Being too early could get us shot.

Oh, be on the lookout for a semi-truck that will run. That would make bringing supplies home much easier.

Harold will lead one team, and I'd like Greg to lead another while Jack builds our Great Wall of the Horseshoe."

"If it's okay, I'll take Ned with me on my team. My two sons will round out my team," replied Harold.

Greg added, "Jack, could you ask Tony to join my team? I'll add Wilma and her husband. They both hunt and could come in handy."

Betty Lou looked at the men and said, "Boys, I need some sleep and so do you. Let's call this a day and start the fun again in the morning."

95

*

Chapter 6

Day Two – Friend or Foe

Will rolled over and wrapped his arms around the girl as he slept. The thief had knocked her out the night before when she tried to run them off. It was barely daylight, and the sun had not peeked above the horizon.

Jake stirred in his sleep and rolled over on a rock, which woke him from a sound sleep. He rubbed his eyes and saw his brother cuddled up to a pretty dark haired girl with a gash on her head and dried blood on her face.

"Grandma! Grandma, wake up!"

Jane lay there trying to sleep a few more minutes when she heard Jake. She rolled over and propped herself up on her elbow and signaled for him to be quiet. Jake waved and pointed at the girl.

"What the hell? Where did she come from?"

Jane crawled over to Will and gently shook him until he woke up. He yawned and tried to stretch, but the girl had his arm trapped below her. She was snoring and sound asleep. Will signaled to his Grandma that he didn't know what was going on with the girl.

Jane crawled over to the other side and saw the girl had a wound on her head and said, "Will this girl has been hit on the noggin. Did you go out last night and bring a girl back to camp."

"No. The first time I saw her was when I woke up."

"With your hand on her chest."

"No! I was asleep."

"I need to check her out. She hit her head, or someone hit her. Jake, go fetch me the First Aid Kit, a clean T-shirt and a bottle of water."

Jake walked over to their supplies, fetched the shirt and water, and returned to his Grandma. He handed her the items when suddenly his head snapped back to his left, and he yelled, "The bikes are gone!"

Will ran up the slope and saw tire tracks and footprints heading toward the highway. He also found a trail of blood that he lost when the tracks got to the road. It bothered him that the blood trail ended heading in the direction they were going to go shortly. He was mad and shook as he thought about the bastards sneaking into their camp while all were asleep. He looked down and saw he had his pistol in his hand. That was the moment that he knew it was kill or be killed in this new dangerous world.

Will walked back down the hill to the camp and saw his Grandma cleaning the blood from the young girl's head. The gash was on the top of her head as though someone had clubbed her. Jane had cleaned the area, applied an antibiotic, and a bandage. The wound was above her hairline so it would be hidden.

"Grandma, I think this girl scared the thieves away. There is a blood trail leading up to the highway and a rock with blood on it where we parked our bikes. I think she tried to scare them away and got clubbed for her effort," Will said.

"Good guess," they heard the girl mumble.

"Child, don't move. You've been hit in the head."

"I was wondering why my head hurt so much. Have you got any aspirin?"

"Yes dear. Missy, fetch two aspirin and some more water. Now tell us what happened."

The girl tried to sit up but slumped back down and said, "I was tired and was asleep under the other overpass when you came down the hill to camp. I didn't think you were a threat, so I went back to sleep. Something woke me up in the middle of the night and I saw several guys stealing your bikes. I yelled at them and threw a rock. I hit one in the head and knocked his ass to the ground. One of the guys ran over with a club and swung it at me. I deflected the blow with my arm, but the club still hit me on my head. That's all I remember."

"There was no telling what those men had in mind. You saved us from whatever they planned," Jane replied.

"They stole your bikes. That's what they planned. It was a bunch of high school kids, and I'll bet I know them. We were on buses heading up to Mammoth Cave on a field trip from school in Lebanon when the buses and all electronics died. There were about 80 of us counting the professors. My Mom and three kids were killed when our driver lost control and hit a dump truck."

"What's your name?"

"Maddie O'Berg and I'm from a small town east of Nashville, Lebanon, Tennessee."

Maddie, I know Lebanon, and I have been there many times. It's not far out of our way, and we can drop you off with your father. Is he Senator O'Berg?"

"My dad died a long time ago. My Mom and I have been on our own for almost six years. He was a jerk and very mean to my Momma. I hated him. Can I go with you to where you are going?"

Missy spoke first, "Will would like that."

Will slapped her on the back of her head and asked his Grandma, "Can she come with us to the Horseshoe?"

"I'm 17 and will be eighteen in October. I'm a good worker."

Jane thought for a minute and replied, "Certainly you can come with us. You risked your life to help us, and you are a good person. You will have to pull your own weight and help with chores to live with us. If you come with us, you have to do what I say when I say until you are 18 and then you are free to stay with the community or leave."

"I'm okay with all of that. I'm a good worker and will do my part. What are your names?"

"I'm Jane Carter, and I'm the kid's Grandmother, and my husband died years ago. This is Will, Missy, and Jake Karr. My daughter is their mother, and we are heading to their Grandfather's home about twenty miles east of Lebanon. Their mother is a policewoman, and their father is a Nurse Practitioner."

"Pleased ta' meet ya' Jane, Will, Missy, and Jake. Does your Grandfather have room for all of us?"

"Yes, he does, and we will make more space when we get there," Will chimed in, and then asked, "What grade were you in in school?"

"I was a senior and studying to get ready to become a Pediatrics Doctor. I've always wanted to become a doctor and help little kids. What about you?"

"I'm a junior and studying to prepare to go into law enforcement like my Mom. I want to go to law school and then become an FBI agent."

Will and Maddie wandered away from the others while getting to know each other. Jane made the other two start breaking camp and after a short while yelled for the other two to help. Maddie went to get her things and came back with her backpack, sleeping bag, a rifle, and food all neatly stacked in a pushcart.

"Where did you find the cart and rifle?"

"A sporting goods store about a mile from here. They had several more. The clerk took $200 cash in exchange for the cart and the rifle. We can go get another one if you want."

"Will, here is $300 in tens and twenties. Try to haggle him down if possible. I'll stay with Missy and Jake. You two hustle and get back quickly."

Will checked his pistol and covered it with his shirt. They headed back into Glasgow and only walked about half a mile before they saw several fires and looters robbing many of the stores. Men and women were screaming at each other and fighting over shopping carts piled with food.

"That looks like a bunch of Zombies fighting for their next meal."

"Yeah, let's get in and out without attracting any one's notice."

They walked on to the sporting goods store and found it ransacked. There were no guns or ammo visible and the manager was lying dead behind the counter.

"Oh shit, that's the man who sold me the stuff."

"Hey, there's one of those carts. Grab sleeping bags while I look for anything else we might need," said Will.

He scrounged around the area behind the counter and found a Ruger .357 Magnum, several boxes of .357, two boxes of .22 ammo and a loaded pump 12 Gauge shotgun. Will checked and it was loaded with Double Aught Buckshot. He looked for more ammo without any luck. He found several Bowie knives and hatchets under the mess on the floor.

Maddie had also found some useful items during her search. She had placed three sleeping bags, a small hiking tent, two Swiss Army knives, and a pile of freeze-dried food packages in the cart.

They were prepared to leave when Maddie spotted something behind the counter in the corner. It was a compound bow. She fetched it and placed it in the cart.

"Help me look for some hunting arrows. You know the pointy ones with the sharp blades."

"I know what a hunting arrow looks like. My Papaw and I hunt for deer every season. Look, there's a turned over rack of arrows."

They took three big handfuls of arrows and two boxes of arrowheads and placed them in the cart.

Will said, "Maddie, let's sneak out the back door and go down the alley until we have to make a break for the highway. I'm placing the shotgun on top along with your rifle. We may have to use them if someone tries to take our stuff."

They snuck out the back door and made it to the highway before being noticed by a group of men leaving a gas station with clubs in their hands.

The people began to run towards them when Will said, "Maddie, take the cart and go as fast as you can to the others. I'll stay and slow these assholes down."

"No Will Karr. I'm also fighting."

They aimed their weapons and fired a shot above the crowd's heads to no avail. Will lowered the shotgun, fired straight at the rushing men, and hit several. They screamed and dropped to the ground holding their legs since Will's shot was aimed low. Will threw the shotgun in the cart and they took off as fast as Will could push the cart. The men didn't follow them. Maddie kept looking back to make sure they weren't followed and was relieved when they arrived at the overpass to see the others on the road and ready to leave.

"What was the gunfire?"

"Some men started to chase us, and we changed their minds with a load of buckshot. I didn't kill any of them, but several will need buckshot removed.

Maddie here is a loaded .22 Ruger pistol. Missy, you take my 12 Gauge pump. I'll take the other 12 Gauge and the .357 Magnum it kicks, but I've shot Papaw's .45 Colt, and I can handle the kick back."

Jane spoke up, "Missy, keep the barrel pointed away. Jack a round into the chamber, and then put another round in the feed tube. Now push the safety on. Leave it on unless we are attacked. Take the safety off, place the butt securely against your shoulder, point and pull the trigger. It will kick like a mule, but if you keep it pressed against your shoulder, it won't hurt you."

They loaded the rest of their stuff on the second cart and headed south. They were pushing the cart at a fast walking pace and trading up pushing the cart every half hour with Missy and Jake both pushing the same cart when it was their turn.

"Grandma, we need to pick up the pace and travel at a fast jog if we are ever going to get to Grampa's."

"Will I think you are right, but what we really need is a vehicle or some horses. Everyone keep your eyes peeled for horses, tractors or an old car that looks like it will run."

Highway 31E had numerous small businesses and subdivisions along their route, and they found that people were trying to get them to stop and talk. The folks were starving for information about what happened and sought to speak with every stranger who passed by. They found themselves stopped and trying to get away from talkative people more than a dozen times before noon. They found a long stretch of deserted highway and stopped for lunch off the road out of sight.

Maddie looked at Will and said, "Mrs. Carter, we need to make sure we take the shortest route possible down to the Horseshoe. Were you planning to take 31E most of the way or the back roads? I've driven or rode on all of these roads for years."

"Maddie, you can call me Jane. I was going to take 31E down to a few miles north of Lebanon and then cut east to Dixon Springs which is just a couple of miles north of the Horseshoe."

"Grandma, Maddie is right. We need to switch to a southeast course along these roads," Will said as he pointed to the map.

"Maddie, you take over the navigation."

"At the rate, we are going we can make Mr. Karr's place in two and a half to three days. We're only 40 to 45 miles from there right now. We'll cut off 31E at Highway 87."

They continued their trek after lunch and were soon at the Highway 87 junction.

"Grandma, look that garage has a bunch of old tractors for sale," Jake said then added, "I'll bet he has a wagon also. We could ride down to Papaw's home."

"It's worth a try. I don't know if we have anything to trade that's worth a tractor."

They walked up to the garage and started looking at the tractors when a loud voice said, "You want to buy a tractor?"

Will replied, "Do you have any that will still run?"

"All of these run. I'll take silver, gold, diamonds, or other trade goods that catch my fancy."

"Will you take cash?"

The man broke out laughing and replied, "Toilet paper is all cash is now."

Jane took her engagement ring off her finger, showed it to the man, and said, "This was worth $10,000 a few years back. Will it buy a tractor?"

"Let me see it."

He pulled out a jewelers loop, examined the stone, and then walked over to his garage and scratched a window with it.

"I'll trade you that garden tractor for it."

"Oh no! That's too small, and my ring is worth that large one on the other end."

"Hell no! In a week I can get a hundred thousand dollars for that tractor."

"Remember you said money is worthless. I'll take the middle one and a wagon to pull the kids and our gear with."

"Maybe, can you sweeten the offer?"

Maddie took her necklace off, handed it to the man, and said, "This diamond is worth all of your tractors. Give her ring back, and we'll make the deal."

The man looked at the large diamond and then scratched the glass one more time before handing Jane her ring.

"Now that's a deal. I'll even throw in a full tank of gas, a siphon hose, and hook the wagon to the tractor."

The wagon was just large enough for the four passengers so Will used bailing wire to attach the carts to the back of the trailer. Then he made a holder for the shotgun from a piece of PVC pipe, and they were ready to go.

The tractor was a 1950 Ford 8N that had been restored many years back but was still in good shape. Will jumped into the driver's seat, started it, and let it warm up.

"Grandma, tractors can go about 15-20 MPH. We can run safely at about 10-12 MPH with this old tractor. That means we would arrive at Papaw's house after dark. I think we get close to his house and then go on in the morning."

"Good thinking. There is a small city just above the Horse Shoe, Dixon Springs, I think. We will find a place in the woods and then travel to Bob's house early before most people are up. Knowing Bob, he will already be up.

Kids, have your guns ready. This tractor will get a lot of attention. Most folks are great people, but you have already seen that good people will steal to save their lives."

"Okay, the tractors ready, hang on," Will said as they lurched into motion."

As expected, many people waved at them, and a few tried to get the tractor to stop. Will and Jane had already agreed that they weren't stopping for anyone. Jane told the kids that their lives meant more to her than any stranger's life and there wasn't any extra room in the wagon. She told Will, off by himself, to shoot anyone who attempted to stop them or take the tractor.

They drove for a little over an hour and only had to dodge a few mad people who demanded that they stop and give them a ride.

Jane saw something dart off the road and into the bushes up ahead and yelled, "Stop! Something's wrong up ahead. Girls keep your weapons handy. Will and I are going to scout up ahead. There might be an ambush. Will, follow me."

Jane stepped down from the wagon and walked into the bushes and trees on the left side of the road. She waved at Will to keep the noise down.

"Will, I thought I saw someone trying to hide up ahead about a hundred feet or so on the left side of the road. Let's sneak up there and see what's going on. Be ready to shoot."

Will followed his Grandma and wondered how his Grandma had so quickly changed into this fearless leader tromping through the woods with a rifle ready to shoot people. His Mom had been a cop for as long as he could remember, but his Grandma had always been the Country Club type playing tennis and golf. When his Grampa died, she sold the house on the 18 hole at the Country Club and moved to Clermont to a much smaller home. She also went to nursing school and became an RN.

Jane motioned for him to stop and Will froze in his tracks. Jane covered her lips with her index finger and motioned for Will to come up beside her. There ahead in the woods was a small camp with two tents, a couple of beat up old cars and piles of trash, clothes, and luggage.

It was obvious that these people were robbing anyone who passed by on the road. One of the tents was moving, and Jane heard voices. There was a muffled scream from a man, and then a gunshot.

"That bitch won't bite anymore," yelled a man from the tent. Son, bring me the red head."

"Will, walk up to the tent and shoot the man in the tent. I'll take the son and any others."

Will looked at her with a dumb look, and then moved toward the tent. He looked in through a screen window and saw the man nursing a bloody spot on his arm. Will took a deep breath, opend the flap and shot the man in the stomach with the .357. The bullet knocked the man backward, and he fell against the back of the tent, which knocked it down. Will stood outside and saw a man walking up behind his Grandma who had just shot one man and was about to shoot another.

"Lookout," Will said as he shot the man twice in the chest as Jane shot the last man standing.

Jane looked around for any other dangers while Will untied the three women and a young boy. The women were grateful to be free but then were horrified to see only four dead men.

"There are two more around here. They were sneaking up the road to attack someone riding on a tractor."

Jane and Will ran as fast as they could up the road to the tractor, but gunfire came from that direction, and Jane thought the worst had happened. They headed into the woods the last hundred feet to have some cover as they advanced to the tractor. The shooting stopped as quickly as it started and Will prepared himself for a gun battle.

There was no battle since there were two dead men on the ground and Missy and Maddie were reloading their guns.

"What happened?"

"We got out of the wagon and hid in the woods. Those nasty men came up yelling for us to get out of the wagon and we shot them," said Maddie. I shot the young one, and Missy got the old fart with the beard and rotten teeth."

"And I helped," said Jake."

'What did Grandma's big boy do?"

"I threw a rock and hit the old fart on the head to let the girls sneak up on them. They shot at the trees but didn't get close to me because Maddie told me to throw the rock and duck behind the log."

"I'm proud of all of you. For a bunch of city people, we done good."

Will looked at his Grandma and said, "Grandma, you looked like an Army platoon leader as you directed me up to their camp. Then you outshot the bad guys in a firefight."

"Will, this ain't this girl's first rodeo."

"What does that mean?"

"Your mom isn't the first female cop in the family?"

All three of her Grandkids replied at the same time, "What?"

"I'll tell you a story after we get to your Papaw's house."

They went on down to the thug's camp to check on the women and found they had buried their friend and were loading their belongings into one of the old cars.

"Thanks for freeing us from those creeps. We're heading home to Glasgow. We can never repay you for your help, but if you ever make it to Glasgow, you'll always have a meal and a place to stay."

They traveled on for about 11 miles before Will waved back to the others and yelled, "Look up ahead."

An RV was set up just as though the occupants were camping. There were six men and women plus several children milling around the RV. Will saw that the RV was in the middle of the road and the tractor could barely get past it on the right side. As they approached several of the people started pointing at the approaching tractor, and then several began waving.

Will kept the tractor moving and actually sped up when suddenly a man jumped out in front of the tractor. Will didn't stop, and the tractor ran over the man crushing him. Will kept moving until shots rang out just as he got beside the RV. Will aimed the .357 at the closest man with a gun, aimed, squeezed the trigger, and blew a large hole in the man's chest. The other man got off a wild shot with a snub-nosed .38 but missed Jane by several feet. He shot again before Jane put a .30 .30 round into his stomach and another into his shoulder. Maddie shot twice and hit the same man Will killed. Missy never pulled her trigger.

One of the women ran up with a pistol while trying to shoot at Will. She kept pulling the trigger; however, nothing happened. The gun had jammed. Will jumped off the tractor slugged the woman and took the silenced Ruger MKIII pistol from her. The other two women were crying and screaming. Jane looked at the pistol and stuck it into her waistband.

"You killed my husband. He was a policeman. You killed three policemen."

Jane fired her .30 .30 in the air and yelled, "Shut the fuck up. Those men were going to steal our tractor, and they shot first. They tried to kill my Grandson. Screw them and screw you."

She saw the New York license plate on the front of the RV and said, "Get your Yankee asses back to New York. We're coming back through here tomorrow, and if we see you, we'll shoot you on sight and give the kids to honest people.

Son let's go!"

Will put the tractor in gear and drove them off at a high rate of speed.

Maddie yelled, "Missy has been shot."

Jane looked over at Missy and saw her slumped down against Maddie. She checked her and saw a red stain on her shoulder.

"Missy, are you okay?"

Missy was unconscious but alive. Jane waved at Will to keep going as she and Maddie tended to Missy's wound. She dug a package of Wound Seal out of Will's Bugout Bag and a large bandage. She poured the Wound Seal into the wound and applied pressure. The bleeding stopped. They made Missy as comfortable as possible.

Jane yelled, "Will, speed up some and drive straight to your Grandfather's home.

The next 20 miles took over three hours due to the rough dirt and gravel roads that had to be taken to save time. They arrived at Dixon Springs at sundown and just waved at people as they cut off on Rome Rd, which led to their Papaw's home. They had only traveled a short distance out of Dixon Springs when there was a roadblock ahead.

"Who are you and why are you heading south on this road," the guard at the roadblock challenged."

"I'm Bob Karr's Grandson, and my sister has been shot we need to get to my Papaw's home."

"Move the barricade. I'm Greg Farmer. I'll take you to Bob's home."

Greg hopped on a nearby ATV and took off down the road while keying the mic on his radio, "Bob, this is Greg."

"Hey, Greg. How's it hanging?"

"Not good. Bob, your Grandkids arrived, and one has been hurt. I'm bringing them to your house, and several of the ladies are coming to help."

"Oh shit. I'll clear the table and set up some lights."

Bob frantically retrieved his first aid supplies, several Coleman, and electric lanterns and placed several blankets and a pillow on his kitchen table. He placed a large pan of water on his Coleman stove and lit the burner. He was as ready as possible with only a few minutes warning.

Bob waited on his front porch, and in a few minutes, Greg arrived on his ATV followed by a tractor pulling a wagon. He recognized Jane and his Grandkids but noticed another girl about Will's age get out of the wagon.

"Greg, help me carry Missy into the house. Kids sorry I can't hug you until we take care of Missy."

They carried her into the kitchen and laid her on the table. Jane cut her t-shirt away to expose the wound and then swabbed the area with alcohol.

Some alcohol got into the wound and Missy came to and screamed, "Damn that hurts. What happened?"

Jane replied, "Dear one of those men shot you in the shoulder. Don't worry. It will hurt like Hell, but you will be okay and back to normal in a few weeks. Here take these two pain pills so we can examine the wound."

The Hydrocodone worked quickly, and Missy was very drowsy. Greg and Bob held Missy down while Jane probed for the bullet with a pair of forceps. She found the bullet and dropped it onto the table.

"That's a .22 caliber bullet. Kinda light for attacking someone," Bob stated.

Jane used her elbow to point at the Ruger in her waistband. Bob pulled it out and said, "Damn, this is what certain people use to kill people up close and personal like a hitman."

"A woman tried to shoot Will with it, and we assumed the safety was on. It actually jammed, and that saved Will from the same fate."

She took the pistol back and said, "It's mine now."

Bob replied, "Are you sure you want that gun?"

"Bob, I'm sure. I like .22s," Jane said as she squirted some antibiotic on Missy's wound. She kept pressure on the wound and then wrapped the wound with a bandage that kept pressure on the wound.

"Okay. You saw that the bullet was only about an inch deep. The gun had subsonic rounds in it. It's probably been reworked to allow the gun to cycle those low recoil low-velocity bullets. I think you killed some pretty bad people back there."

Will said, "The woman said the three men were cops."

"I call bullshit on that. The soccer mom then tried to use a silenced .22 to kill my family. Double bullshit. If we didn't have more important things to do, I'd go back and kill both of those women," replied Jane.

They placed Missy in bed and took turns watching her and her wounded shoulder the rest of the night.

"Grandma, I've never seen you this mad," said Will.

"Son, those people tried to kill my Grandkids. That pissed me off. I'm sorry for making an ass of myself."

"No Grandma, you kept us alive. I've never seen you this mad. I saw you miss a three-foot eagle putt and you just shrugged it off."

"I'll be back to normal now that my kids are safe."

"Greg, this is Jane who is my son's mother in law. These three are Missy, Jake, and Will my Grandkids."

112

Jane spoke up and said, "This is Maddie O'Berg, and she is from Lebanon. She saved us from robbers, and we kinda adopted her along the way."

"Maddie are you related to Senator O'Berg from Lebanon?"

"He might be a distant relative. No, it was just mom and me at home and Mom died in the bus wreck."

Bob hugged his Grandkids and asked, "Have you heard anything from your Mom or Dad?"

Will answered, "No sir. We headed down here right after hanging the phone up with you and had some trouble along the way. Papaw, you wouldn't believe how Grandma kept us safe and kept us marching to get here."

"Your Grandma is a lot like your Mom. They are both tough and amazing ladies. Nothing they do would surprise me."

Jane made a sign to Bob by placing her finger over her lips.

They all talked on the front porch for several hours with Jake fast asleep with his head on Jane's lap. Bob's house had three bedrooms, and his gooseneck travel trailer was a bunkhouse style that slept eight.

"Jane you can sleep in the first bedroom on the right going down the hall. Bill and Jo get the one on the right at the end of the hall and mine is the one on the other side. Maddie, you get the bed over the gooseneck in my trailer; Will, you get the bed on the other end of the trailer, and Jake gets the kitchen table that makes into a bed. Missy gets the couch. This will have to do until we sort things out."

Jane added, "Let's all get a good night's sleep and in the morning we will figure out our long-term plans."

"There are plenty of towels, wash clothes, and soap in the trailer, but we don't have hot water. I'd take a who.... Well, a... Just wipe yourselves down tonight, and I'll heat some water up in the morning for a proper hot bath."

The kids headed to the trailer and Jane looked in on Missy before returning to the porch.

Bob handed Jane a tumbler with three fingers of whiskey and said, "Ya' done good. I can't thank you enough for getting the kids down here. A toast to our other kids. May they find the way down less troublesome than their kids did?"

They touched glasses and drank the drink to the bottom of the glass. Bob poured three fingers in both glasses and took a sip.

Jane looked at her glass and said, "Why Bob are you trying to get me drunk and take advantage of me?"

"Jane, no man could ever take advantage of you. I was hoping you'd take advantage of me."

"Bob, I like you, but I don't want to start anything until I know Jo and Bill are safe. I am worried to death about them. I'm thinking about heading north to find them."

"If they don't arrive in two days, I'll go with you. If you change your mind, my door will always be open."

Jane sat on the porch for a while longer and thought about her future. Sure, she'd thought about hooking up with Bob a year or so after her husband died, but she wasn't sure she wanted a full-time man in her life right now. She thought back to the attacks on the kids and her and the many people that had been raped, killed, or robbed and her blood boiled.

She also wondered if that traitor O'Berg had been stuck in D.C. or was at his home in Lebanon when the shit hit the fan. Her mind moved to Maddie and wondered why she hated her dad, the Senator so much. Maddie was born during the investigation, and Jane still had a copy of O'Berg's file. She was certain that he was a Russian mole in the US Senate. She hated the bastard.

Jane sat on the edge of the bed making mental notes about what she wanted to accomplish during the next five days. She fell asleep adding to the list.

*

Chapter 7

Day Two – Walt's Plan

Walt had always planned to head out to Western Kentucky to live if the shit hit the fan. His ex-wife and kids lived below Owensboro in a small community called Pleasant Ridge. Walt's third crime in two days was stealing an old pickup from an automotive museum in Louisville. He walked into an auto parts store and made the manager give him a hand pump and hose so he could steal gas from stalled cars.

He shot a clerk and two looters in a Walmart parking lot to take their grocery carts full of food. He then went back to the gun shop where he and Jo had killed the robbers and found it empty. He drove on to a pawnshop that had two guards out front defending the store. Since he was in uniform, the guards allowed him to get too close. That was a deadly mistake for them. Walt shot them, took an AK47 from one of the dead guards, and used it to rob the pawnshop.

He now had enough food, weapons, ammo, and water to head west. He decided to take the northern route across lower Indiana to avoid people as much as possible. Highway 64 had heavy traffic around Louisville but very few cities close to the road itself. The drive was very frustrating because people kept trying to stop him to get a ride. He crossed the median several times to whip around them but finally just ran over the next two groups. He decided this was a mistake when one woman bounced into the windshield and cracked the passenger side glass.

He continued on east weaving between stalled cars and people begging for a ride or needing help. He began laughing at them and even shot a few unlucky ones. He was passing by Ferdinand when several policemen tried to stop him to confiscate his truck. He slowed down and honked for them to get out of the way. When they didn't, he stuck the AK out the window, shot all three of them, and then calmly drove on.

Walt had become a sociopath and had no feeling at all about killing the men and women along the way. His world had ended when the shit hit the fan and Jo left him for her wuss of a husband.

He was on a mission to make his ex-wife and kids love him again and live with them the rest of his life. He cut off onto the highway and was on the final leg to his family. There were only a few stalled cars and trucks along this divided highway once he got away from Louisville, so he made good time to the Highway 231 Exit. He headed south to Owensboro and drove across the bridge to Owensboro. He had to stop several times to push stalled cars out of his way and to stop people from trying to force him to give them rides.

There were cars and trucks stalled all the way through Owensboro. Again, several people tried to get him to stop, and several were shot for their effort. He was on a mission and didn't have time for idiots stranded on the highway or their injured families. It took two hours to get to the south side of Owensboro, and he still had to go 12 miles to get to his old home. He saw the sign up ahead for Highway 764 and made the left turn at 50 MPH whizzing past several people waving for help.

He drove on about four miles and made a left turn on Cotton Lane. His house was the one at the end of the lane on the left. His family had owned the land for over 200 years. They had sold off over a thousand acres, but he had about six hundred when the bitch filed for divorce. She got the house and a hundred acres in the settlement. He kept the remaining acreage for hunting since it was about 50 percent farmland and 50 percent dense woods. He rented the farmland out to a local farmer and used that money to pay the taxes on the land.

He saw the house on the left, and there wasn't anyone outside. He parked in the driveway and got out of the car while watching for people. The nearest house was over 500 yards back around a bend in the road so there shouldn't be anyone around. He was looking in the window with his pistol drawn when he heard a vehicle approaching from behind him. It was a man driving a John Deere Gator, and he had a rifle across his lap.

Walt recognized his neighbor Tom Wathen just as he was ready to shoot this intruder.

"Walt, is that you?"

"Tom, it's me, Walt Long. How's it hanging old buddy?"

"Not so well since the lights went out. I see you have a police uniform on. Where are you living now?"

"Louisville until today. I'm moving back home today."

"Buddy, your ex-wife sold this place a month ago and moved to New York with the kids. I thought you knew."

It was all Walt could do to remain calm. He liked Tom and would not kill him today.

"Why did she move?"

"She married that airline pilot she was dating, and he was based out of JFK. Walt, she was pregnant and due in July according to my wife."

"Who bought the place?"

"West KY Coal. They planned to strip mine the area along with 2,000 additional acres."

"Then they won't mind if I stay in my old home until I figure out what to do with myself."

"Hell, Walt, I don't think the power is ever going to come back on. The Ruskies done nuked our asses."

"Thanks, I need some time alone to work things out in my mind."

Walt broke a window in the side door and entered the house. It still had all of their furniture. He walked up to the fireplace, cried for a few minutes, and then began punching holes in the walls with his fist until his fist was a bloody mess.

He slept for a while until he woke up in a sweat yelling, "Jo. I must get to Jo."

*

Chapter 8

Day Three – The Horseshoe

Bob woke early, as usual, that morning and found Jane in the kitchen making coffee wearing one of his t-shirts and a pair of his old gym shorts. He stopped and stared for a minute, and then walked in and said, "Good morning Jane."

"I saw you sneaking up on me. Bob, I can't thank you enough for allowing me to join your family down here. I don't know what I'd have done otherwise."

"Jane, first it's our family, and second you are one of the strongest ladies I know. You and Jo are cut from the same cloth."

"So you're saying that I'm not very ladylike?"

"Whoa, that's not it. I mean that you are a beautiful lady who can handle any situation and survive."

"Much better. Now, what can this tough old bird do to help our family and community?"

"Jane you are younger than I am and in better shape."

"I noticed you were checking out my shape before you entered the room."

"See, nothing gets past you. Now down to business. I know that you were in law enforcement before you were married but got out of it when you married. I don't know much else about your skill sets besides golf and tennis."

"Well for starters, I'm a licensed fixed wing pilot, scuba diver, and excellent marksman with pistol, rifle, or bow. I can also type and do book keeping but hate the tedious stuff. Oh and I'm a nurse."

"Let's get you with Jack Fulkerson. He is our head of security, and he can figure out how you can assist him with security and training. We have a bunch of people who know how to hunt but nothing about the fine art of killing or pulling guard duty for that matter. Oh, you'll have to double up as a nurse until Bill arrives."

"Great, I was afraid you'd put me mowing the grass or washing dishes."

"We will all pitch in and do those chores."

"Bob, what do you think about Will, Missy, and Maddie joining the security force? All have what it takes to help protect our community. I'd like to start training anyone over 15 to start serving and every child above ten how to handle firearms."

Bob replied, "I like it. We might end up in a fight to the death one day and need every gun we can get."

"Bob, let me get some jeans on, and I'll go with you. Perhaps I can be of some help."

"I have to eat a biscuit and drink a cup of coffee, so don't rush."

Bob and Jane met with Harold and Greg at Greg's house before their teams left out to scrounge for supplies and food.

"I want to give you some advice and one order. The advice is to get as many canned goods and medical supplies as possible on this trip. We may only make a couple of these trips before it gets too hot out there to openly travel on the roads. You will draw a lot of attention, and someone may try to take your vehicles. Now the order. Don't get yourselves killed. Cut and run if you have to get back safely. Don't get in gunfights."

Harrold Hunter had lived in the Horseshoe all of his life except for spending four years in Lexington, Kentucky to go to The University of Kentucky. His fellow Volunteers still gave him shit about that 25 years later. He was 48, divorced with two grown kids and one grandkid. His ex-wife and their kids lived in Dixon Springs, but his two sons and their families moved back home with him a couple of days ago. He invited his ex, but she wouldn't move back home. He had owned the store for a few years.

He volunteered to lead one of the scavenging teams and had his two sons and Ned Kelly on his team. They left Greg's home driving Harold's son's 1973 F100 Ford long bed pickup towing a large horse trailer.

Harold's goal was to go across the Hartsville Bridge and drop down to Highway 40 and look for stalled semi's loaded with food or other necessary supplies. The sun was just coming up, so there wasn't anyone out on the roads, so the trip to Hartsville was uneventful. Driving through Hartville was a different matter. Several people ran out of their houses and tried to flag them down but were too late to catch the old truck. When they slowed to make the turn south onto Highway 141, two policemen waved at them to stop. Harold slowed and then stopped without getting out of the truck.

"Where are you headed and how did you get the truck running?"

Harold replied, "We're heading down to Lebanon to get my sister and her kids to stay with me until the lights come back on."

"What about the truck?"

"Any old truck that doesn't have electronic ignition should run. There should be plenty around here."

"What if we need your truck?"

"We need the truck for Dixon Springs, but we'd be glad to send a mechanic over to help get some of yours running."

"What if someone tries to take the truck away from you," one of the cops said with a nasty grin.

"Boys," Harold said as he raised his pistol and his sons raised their rifles.

"I guess they will die trying to steal our truck. If you don't have anything else, we'll go on our way."

"Y'all have a safe trip."

Greg's team consisted of Tony Fulkerson, Wilma, and her husband George Downs; they drove George's old GMC Suburban and pulled a large cargo trailer. They headed to Highway 25 first then some of the other state highways later to find stalled semis that contained anything useable. Greg decided to head east because he had already emptied three trailers heading to Hartsville and thought they had a better chance toward Carthage.

They only drove a short distance until they saw a semi that had plowed into three cars just before the turn to the racetrack. The driver's body had gone through the windshield, and everyone in the cars was dead. The truck had a sign that said Association of Independent Grocers on the door.

"It looks like a grocery truck. Hope it was delivering and not on the way back to the Distribution Center. George, fetch the bolt cutters."

George walked up and said, "No one locks empty trailers. I think we hit pay dirt."

He cut the lock and opened both doors to expose two full pallets of laundry and cleaning supplies.

"Well, we'll need this stuff to wash the clothes and keep the germs down. Load it up."

Greg backed the cargo trailer up to the back of the semi and lowered the tailgate to match up with the trailer floor. This allowed them to use the two hand trucks they had brought along to speed up loading.

"Wilma, take my AR15 and stand guard while we load this stuff into the trailer."

"Greg, I'd put the bottles of detergent, bleach and other cleaning supplies in the back of the Suburban, so they don't contaminate any food if one gets broken."

"Good idea."

They filled the back of the Suburban with the cleaning supplies and then placed the remainder on the ground. Greg climbed on top of the next pallet of cleaning supplies and yelled down. Now we hit pay dirt. There are canned goods, cereal, and some kind of hygiene or medical supplies further up.

They had been loading for a couple of hours when Wilma yelled, "We've got company. Two men are walking towards us from the race track, and three more think they are sneaking up on us from the woods along the river."

"Grab your guns. Wilma, get your shotgun and give me the AR."

Greg walked to the front of the Suburban and stood behind the front of the vehicle for cover. The two men were fifty feet away when Greg yelled, "That's close enough. What do you want?"

The taller of the two men yelled back, "That's our grocery truck, and we thank you for loading the food into our new Suburban and trailer."

The two men had stringy long hair that hadn't been washed for months and had biker gang jackets on their backs. One had a sawed-off double-barreled shotgun, and the other had a pistol.

Greg whispered to his team. George, you and Tony take out the three in the woods. Wilma, shoot the short one, and I'll shoot the tall asshole. Wait until I shoot.

"My friend, this stuff belongs to us now. If you wanted it, you should have got off your lazy ass and took it before now. Now take your happy ass back to the rock you crawled out from and disappear."

The man started to raise the shotgun when Greg shot him, and then took aim at the second man. He was too late because Wilma's blast of Double Aught Buckshot caught him square in the belly and knocked him back ten feet. Greg heard shots coming from his right and saw Tony and George gunning the other three down. Five bodies lay on the ground.

"George, keep guard while we drag these men to the side of the road. Wilma, please get their guns, ammo and any other things they have that would come in handy."

After the men had been piled up on the racetrack side of the road, Greg hung a sign on the top one that said, "Robbers and Killers."

Wilma placed two shotguns, a 9mm pistol, and three .38 snub nose revolvers in the backseat floor.

Greg saw the pile and said, "Thank God these creeps didn't have any serious hardware."

"They only had a few rounds of ammo each. I think they wanted our guns and ammo more than the food."

They finished loading the trailer to the roof and headed back to the Horseshoe after Greg placed his own lock on the trailer. They made two more trips to the trailer that day, but it was empty when they arrived for their final load.

Greg saw his broken lock on the ground and said, "I hope it was good people who took the food. I can't blame them. Let's drive on down the road apiece and see what we can find."

Harold drove the old GMC away from the two cops as fast as the old truck would pull the trailer. They traveled down Highway 141 and only saw one small straight truck that delivered fresh vegetables to quick pick stores, but it was empty. They got off 141 and took backroads south to State Road 24, and headed east toward Carthage.

There were more stalled cars and trucks on this road since it was a straight line between Lebanon and Carthage.

They had only driven a mile before Ned said, "Look up ahead. There are several people beside that straight truck. It's a grocery truck. I guess they have already claimed the food."

The people saw the old pickup and started waving for Harold to stop. There were two men and three women, and all were dressed in business suits and nice dresses. Harold told his team to have their guns ready because he was going to stop.

"Can you give us some food and water? We've been stuck on this road for three days.

Harold told his boys to hand them five bottles of water and said, "Where are y'all from?"

A woman spoke up, "Those two are from Austin, and the rest of us are from Sacramento."

"California?"

"Of course California."

"Hey, Sacramento, Kentucky is only about a hundred miles northwest of here. What do y'all do for a living?"

"We work for a Chinese company that makes computers for all of the major computer companies."

Harold motioned for his son to cut the lock off the truck and said, "I knew y'all weren't from around here because people with common sense would have walked to Carthage or Lebanon by now instead of starving to death with a truckload of food beside them."

Harold opened the door, and the truck only had four pallets of food and several stacks of empty pallets. There was a pallet of Gatorade and a pallet of Spam at the back of the truck.

"Hell, that's enough to feed you five for a month."

"We don't eat that stuff."

"Then you won't mind if we load it up and get it out of your way."

"We'll take a couple of cases of the Gatorade."

Harold dropped several cases of the blue Gatorade at their feet, and a case of bacon flavored Spam and said, "You get real hungry, and you'll eat the Spam.

"You can drop us off at the Nashville Airport. We need to catch flights home."

"Lady, are you blind or just plain loco? There are no more planes flying. Most cars won't run. Hell, your damned computers won't work. There has been an EMP blast or nuclear bomb set off high in the sky, and it fried all electronics. Welcome to 1850 America."

"Where are the police? Someone has to take us to Nashville and feed us."

"Lady, didn't you hear me, or are you as dumb as a box of rocks."

The woman dropped to her knees and started crying. Her world of high technology had disappeared in a flash and had gone for her lifetime.

"We're heading toward Carthage and can drop you off a couple of miles from town if you would like."

One of the men replied, "That would be great."

The woman snapped back, "Charles, we are going to Nashville, and that is the end of the discussion."

The man replied, "Look bitch. I quit. Our company doesn't exist anymore. Who's with me?"

The other man and a woman joined Harold's sons in the back of the pickup and Harold drove off and left the two women mad and cursing.

It was only six miles over to Carthage, but Harold's goal was a sporting goods store on this side of the river. Harold pulled into the store's parking lot and stayed close to the street. He didn't want to spook the owner. He stopped the truck and then pointed to Carthage. The man and woman took their bags that were now filled with Spam and Gatorade and walked toward the bridge to Carthage.

Harold raised his hands in the air and walked toward the sporting goods store's front door. He saw movement through the windows, and soon a man poked a shotgun out the door, aimed it at him, and said, "What the hell do you want?"

"We need some guns and ammo. I have some silver to trade."

"Don't need any silver. Go away."

"Do you need food?"

"What kind of food do you have?"

"Can goods, canned meat, and Gatorade."

"Tell your friends to lay their guns in the back of the pickup, and we'll take a look at your food."

An older man, a young man, and a girl came out of the shop armed with shotguns. The young man had a Keltek KSG 12 Gauge that held 14 rounds. The girl had an AR. They walked up to the truck, and Harold pointed to the back of the trailer.

He lowered the ramp exposing the boxes of food and Gatorade. The three now had smiles on their faces.

"We're short on food, and the Gatorade could come in handy. What do you want?"

"We need ARs, 9mm pistols, shotguns, magazines, and ammo."

"Whoa, son. You ain't got enough food to get all of that. I'll take all of the food and give you two ARs and one each of the others with a hundred rounds for each gun."

"That's a deal. Would you take fresh meat or more groceries for more guns and ammo?"

"What are you trying to do, build an army?"

"Look man. I don't know what you know about our situation, but we are in for some bad times. The looting in the big cities has started. Hell, look over your shoulder even Carthage has several fires burning out of control. It's just a matter of time before the criminals try to steal all of your guns and our food. Why don't you move in with us? We farm all of the land in the Horseshoe and will have plenty of food if we can hold the land from the gangs."

"No, we have a place out in eastern Tennessee, and we are leaving as soon as we finish loading the rest of the guns. If you can deliver the extra food, I'll trade more guns."

"Could you meet us at the bottom of the Horseshoe and we could bring the food across in boats. By the time we drive all the way back and get back here, you will be long gone."

"Yes, but we will be leaving at 4:00 pm sharp. What time do you want to meet us by the river?"

"Okay, we'll be on your side of the river at 3:00 by the Highway 24 Bridge across that big creek."

"Be there on time, or we'll be gone."

They traded all of the food for the weapons and left to hightail it back home. One of Harold's sons reminded Harold that he could use one of the walkie-talkies to contact Bob when they got to the bottom of the Horseshoe.

"Damn great idea," Harold replied.

He called for Bob but got Betty Lou on the walkie-talkie. He told her the situation and asked her to relay the info to Bob so he could round up two boats, the trade goods, and men to row the boats across the river. Betty Lou contacted Bob an hour later, and he got several of the team selecting the trade goods and fetching two boats. They even found one with an old Johnson Outboard that ran.

Harold headed back to Highway 141 and warned the team that the trip back through Hartsville might get a bit dicey. This time everyone had an AR with several shotguns ready in case needed.

The ride back to Hartville was touch and go with several groups trying to get them to stop. Harold actually had to run through a barricade while the others trained their ARs on armed men. A running truck with a trailer looked too tempting to some of the fine law abiding citizens of the area. Running low on food made for desperate and dangerous people.

Harold drove across the bridge and quickly saw that a barricade had been set up on this end of town, and he saw the same cops manning this checkpoint. He pulled up to the sawhorses and stopped.

"Could y'all move the saw horses so we can get back home?"

"No, the Police Chief wants all people that travel through Hartsville to check in at the police station and tell him why you need to travel through our town."

"Look, we have three ARs and a 9mm trained on the two of you. Move the sawhorses, or I'll gun the motor and knock you and them out of the way. Boys shoot to kill if these want to be cops go for their guns."

The two cops moved the barricade while mumbling, "The Chief ain't going to like this. There are three more barricades on your way home. You will be in jail tonight."

"Tell him we'll stop in and see him on the next trip."

"Damn, I'm turning east on the next backroad, and we'll go around Hartsville altogether. By the time they figure it out, we'll be far away from the city."

Bob and Jack had been busy that morning helping a crew string barbwire across the top of the Horseshoe. Jane pitched in and dug holes with the post hole digger, pounded t posts and

131

strung wire just as the men did all day. They placed two six-inch wooden posts every 60 feet and fastened them together with 2x6 boards to give a strong and tight fence. They pounded t posts in every 10 feet between the large posts. Bob insisted that they place red or orange flags between every post on the top wire. He didn't want a horse or deer to be maimed.

"Jack we have eight men...err...people pounding t post and four digging and setting the wooden posts. We should have this done by tomorrow night," said Bob.

"And one woman who works more than any two of the men. Tomorrow let's keep the scavenging teams at home to get this done as soon as possible. What are your plans for a gate and checkpoint?"

"We'll use one of those 16-foot cattle gates and fix wheels on them. The checkpoint will actually be a bunker where our guards can see 360 degrees without being exposed. I'm going over to the old TVA nuke site to borrow some concrete blocks and a shit load of bricks. Greg still has a ton of concrete mix at his store. We'll make a strong guardhouse and bunker. I want to find some body armor for our roving guards. I'm afraid some idiot will take pot shots at us when they figure they can't run us over."

Jane pointed at the numerous stands of trees between the fence and the first farmhouse outside of their community and said, "It's 750 feet from the fence to the nearest farmhouse. If we cut down all of those trees, we get firewood for this winter and an unobstructed field of fire. No one could get across that without being seen."

"Or shot. That also gives any sniper a much longer shot. A good sniper wouldn't have any issue with 250 yards, but most people couldn't hit a bull in the ass with a base fiddle at that range," added Jack.

Bob replied, "Yep. Let's do it. It's a shame we can't find a bulldozer that works."

Jack laughed and said, "Maybe we can."

Bob had to leave to attend to the trade deal, and Jack asked Jane to go with him to the old TVA nuclear plant to see if they could find something to make a more permanent fence for their community.

Jack and Jane rode over to the TVA site in one of the ATVs and took their rifles with them. Jack turned off the road about half a mile before Dixon Springs and cut east across the fields to the abandoned power plant. They drove around the massive industrial park and checked out every business that sprung up at the site after the power plant was scuttled. There were transportation companies, manufacturing, and warehouses.

They found a Tennessee DOT building that had thousands of the steel roadside barriers stacked to the ceiling.

"Jack, we could stick steel posts into the ground and weld these barriers to the posts. Do you have acetylene torches?"

"Yes, but we'll bolt them together and save the gas. That's a great idea. We just need to figure out how to drive the posts into the ground. Let's explore the TVA maintenance and equipment shed," suggested Jack.

Jack opened the man door and found it was pitch black inside. Jane fetched two flashlights from the ATV, and they entered the building. The shed was an enormous building that held the trucks, heavy equipment, and large electrical equipment. The building had a complete machine shop, maintenance bays, and the storage area. They had entered the heavy equipment storage area and then went through several doors to walk through the other sections.

The maintenance area was well lit with skylights. Even the supplies storage area had enough light so that they could walk around without the aid of the flashlights. They went back to the equipment storage area and walked around bulldozers, track hoes, dump trucks, Bobcats, Ditch Witches and a dozen ATVs of all sizes.

"Jack do you think any of this equipment will run. A dozer and a backhoe would come in very handy."

"I doubt it but why let this equipment set here for years only to find out it would run all along."

"How do you start a bulldozer?"

"Pretty much the same as a car; you have to make sure the vehicle is in neutral and blades, buckets, etc. are on the ground. Let's try this dozer."

Jack showed her the forward-reverse lever, the controls for the blade and the ignition, and then tried to start the engine. They were both surprised when the engine started, and black smoke rolled out of the exhaust pipe. Jack shut the engine off since they were in an enclosed building.

"Damn, that's good news. Let's open the overhead doors and get some light in here; this is like a tomb."

"That's why the equipment still runs."

"What?"

"It's a metal building with no windows. It's a perfect Faraday Cage."

It took both of them to pull the chain to raise two of the large doors to open the building up so they could try the engines.

"Damn, we need to get as much of this equipment home as fast as possible before someone else finds it. I'll try the radio."

"Betty Lou. Can you hear me?"

"Yep. Loud and clear. Is everything okay?"

"Yes, all is okay, but we need as many people as can be spared to come up to our location. Load up a pickup and take the route I said I was going to take this morning. This is urgent."

"Okay, that's kinda scary, but I'll get some volunteers."

Jane and Jo started several more of the various types of heavy equipment and then fired up five of the ATVs. Every piece of equipment ran as good as new. Jack then hitched up several dump trucks to the numerous heavy duty trailers and loaded a bulldozer, a track hoe, and eight ATVs onto one trailer. Several pieces of equipment were already on trailers.

Jane said, "Jack, please load that large forklift on a trailer. We can use it to unload the metal to build the wall. There is another in the back corner to load the metal on."

"Great idea."

An hour later a pickup arrived with seven of the fence building team.

"Friends, we have found a treasure trove of heavy equipment that runs. I want you to shuttle all of it back to the Horseshoe for our use, and the extra will be used for trade. I'll show you how to drive the equipment."

Several of the men laughed, one replied, "We all worked in construction at one time or the other over the years. This is a cake walk."

They fired up the dump trucks and one semi, and seven loads were on their way. The pickup followed them to bring them back to the TVA building for the second wave. They made three trips before all of the rolling stock had been delivered. The equipment was spread around to several of the farms, and the entire community was shocked to see the large trucks roll up and deliver the equipment.

Both scavenging teams ended their day successfully and were back home safely before dark. Harold's team did not get back in time to make the trade; however, Bob and several of the community loaded trade food into the boats and traded for 4 - ARs, 6 – 9mm pistols, 3 – 12 Gauge shotguns and a couple of .22 LR Ruger American Rifles with scopes. They also received 1,000 - .223, 1,000 – 9mm, 250 – 12 Gauge, and 5,000 - .22 LR bullets. The trade cost them three boat loads of can goods, medical supplies, and two walkie-talkies. They got a better deal than they deserved since the gun shop owner had more guns than he could possibly need and very little food.

The council met at Bob's house that evening, and the ladies brought potluck for dinner. They ate outside on the front porch and sat on several picnic tables. Their routine was to pray before every meal and another before every meeting. Bob brought the meeting to order and said, "This has been a very successful day for our community and my family. My Grand Daughter Missy is recovering very well; I have my family with me, and our scavenging teams brought home the bacon with the bulldozers and guns. We have half of the fence strung and now have the equipment to construct fortifications that are more permanent.

I must also say that we are way ahead of any reasonable timeframe for getting prepared to survive. Most people don't know the world died two days ago and here we are building a small country. Great job everyone."

Will, Maddie, and Missy sat together a few feet from the meeting and listened intently. Will heard all of the great news but had a frown on his face. He sat there until halfway through the meeting building up the courage to challenge the adults on a fly in the ointment. Will raised his hand and waved it at his Papaw.

"Yes Will, can this wait until the meeting is over?"

"No, sir. With what you just said I have two very important topics for the meeting."

136

"Shoot."

"The one that just came up is that you apparently didn't think that us younger people have any say or contributions to make to the meeting. Please think that over before answering. The three of us have traveled from Northern Kentucky to get here and had to kill several people to protect ourselves. Second and most important, Papaw, the community has violated one of the major rules of post – apocalyptic survival according to my mentor, Bob Karr."

"Bob got a serious look on his face and replied, "Go on son."

"We are bragging about our major accomplishments, two battles, one conflict with the local police, and bringing a dozen large earth moving machines to our community..."

Bob stopped him and said, "Holy shit. You're right. We brought attention to ourselves. Someone or some group noticed every move we made today. We need to be prepared for an attack. Thanks, Will. We are so focused on getting stuff for our survival that we may have placed our families in jeopardy."

That was an eye opener for the group. They discussed the ramifications in detail and asked Bob to appoint a team to put an improved plan together for a low-key effort that yields the same results.

"Will I didn't answer the first issue. You are correct. We adults sometimes don't include teens in meetings and decision-making. Teens will be expected to work as hard as adults, fight and kill beside adults and yes, die beside adults making this community survive and prosper. I don't have an answer now, but you are right to question this as early in this game as possible. I recommend that anyone any age can attend the council meeting and will be allowed to make suggestions regardless of their age."

Everyone agreed, and Betty Lou added this new rule to the charter.

"Now as far as serving on the leadership council, I feel that age is not important. Leadership, wisdom, experience and common sense are what are needed. That means to me that anyone can be nominated to join the council and everyone above 12 years old gets to vote on additions or subtractions to the council. I also think the council should not be larger than seven members."

There was a vote on what Bob recommended, and all of it passed with a yes vote of over 80 percent. A few people didn't think that 13-year-olds should vote; however, they were okay with 13-year-olds fighting and dying to protect their asses.

Betty Lou gave an update on her two assignments. She started with the next targets to scavenge and then read each person's name and skills. She then asked for corrections or additions.

Jane volunteered to assist Betty Lou in the administrative work and was given the perpetual inventory system for the supplies. Jane was given a shoebox with index cards and a pencil.

Maddie raised her hand and said, "I have a couple of ideas on trading with our neighbors for things we need, and that would greatly help them without hurting us. The first is that we can trade the use of some of the earth moving equipment and tractors to local people for trade goods or part of their crops. We could even plow and harvest other community's crops for a share of the crops. We can rent a few of the ATVs to our neighbors for gas or diesel. I'm still brainstorming, but those are the first ideas."

Bob laughed and said, "I like it. Try to make friends of all of our neighbors and make ourselves necessary for their survival. Harold I would like you and Maddie to get three volunteers to start a trading team to figure out how to start a trading system that helps us improve our security and builds a friendship with the communities around us."

Will raised his hand and spoke. He said, "This might fly in the face of what was just said, but I strongly believe that we must actively determine any and all threats to the community and neutralize them as soon as possible."

Greg's wife asked, "Do you mean go out and kill people?"

"Yes, we should kill anyone who we are certain is a threat to this community. I don't mean someone who doesn't like us. I mean biker gangs, drug gangs, and criminals. Those scumbags won't work and will have to rob other people to survive."

Jane added, "Will is correct. My biggest fear is a fifty man MC Club rolls down the road with guns blazing. They could easily get most of those weak minded people above Dixon Springs to join them in attacking us."

Bob saw this wasn't a popular topic so he punted, "Jack, I need you to look into this and give us what we should do to prepare for such a situation."

Will and Jane left the meeting very frustrated.

*

Chapter 9

Day Three – A Long Lonely Road

They slept in until 7:00 am and woke up to find a large breakfast of country ham, fried eggs, hash browns, and pancakes. One of the hostage women helped prepare the breakfast and Jo pitched in to help clean up and wash the dishes before they left. The woman gave them a big piece of country ham and a dozen fried apple pies for the road.

The man fired up a large tractor with a large loader and told them to place their stroller and supplies in the loader and climb in the loader with their stuff so he could take them back up to the road.

Jo said, "Thanks, but we can walk."

"Jo, my plan is to drive you about 15 miles in the direction you were traveling so I could help you make up for lost time."

"That's different. Bill climb in the bucket."

They rode in the bucket for about an hour and a half when the man stopped and lowered the loader to the ground.

"We covered about 20 miles. That should help you get back on schedule."

Jo gave him a hug, and they began their journey well fed, fresh, and eager to head south. The tractor turned around and was soon out of sight. They had run for a while before either of them spoke.

"We are actually ahead of our schedule now. Stopping to help those people helped us," Jo said.

"I'm glad we stopped to help, but it did show me that we have to have wisdom in choosing when to help and when to walk away. We could have been killed last night."

"Hon, they only had two rifles, and we had surprise on our side. I wouldn't have got you into that scrape if I weren't sure of the outcome. My only worry was that one or more of the hostages might have been killed."

"I'll trust your judgment on the criminals and police work if you trust mine on the medical stuff," replied Bill.

"That's a deal. See we make a great team."

"We made a great team last night."

"I'm blushing."

"Run faster, I need to get that off my mind before I beg you to stop."

Jo was happy that Bill and she had made up and were actually acting as if they were in love again. He was kind and considerate as he was before the Walt situation.

141

"Hon, I'm worried about the kids and your Mom. Do you think they have made it to Dad's place yet?"

"Darling my Mom can take care of herself. She taught me most of what I know and can be one tough bitch if needed."

"Jo, I've never seen that side of her. She was always the socialite that threw big parties at their mansion and hung out at the Club playing golf and tennis with the elite."

"That was Dad's world. Mom was a simple farm girl who was a cop when Dad chased her down and married her. She had only been on the job for a year when she broke the case of the Senator's campaign manager taking bribes from the Russian government to influence the vote on the Ukraine. There wasn't enough evidence to convict the Senator, but I know the bastard was guilty."

They had run for a while before Jo said," We have nine hours of daylight left, and we need to be more careful as we run. I will stop at the top of each hill and use the binoculars to scan for danger. Keep an eye out for people, and if necessary we'll head into the woods to walk around any large groups of people."

"Good plan, but the stroller will be a bitch to carry; however, I don't want to have a gang like the one last night get the drop on us."

Bill caught Jo's attention and pointed up ahead to several bodies in the middle of the road.

"Look, there are three young boys."

They cautiously walked up to the boys and saw that two had been shot in the head. Bill rolled the third one over to see if he was alive and the boy moaned. Bill propped the boy's head up and gave him some water. The boy had been shot three times in the chest and once in the leg. It was a miracle he was still alive.

"What happened? Who shot you?"

"We were riding our bicycles, and some men jumped out and pointed a gun at us. They wanted our bikes, food, and water. Demarcus went all macho on them and tried to take the gun from the guy. They struggled, and he shot Demarcus and didn't stop until he shot all of us. I'm going to die aren't I?"

Bill looked at the wounds and replied, "Yes, son, you are going to die."

"I've been good all of my life, but this morning we stole those bikes from an older lady and a bunch of kids. They were sleeping, and we needed the bikes. One woke up and hit Gil on the head. I'm so sorry for that."

The boy's head flopped over, and he died. Jo walked over to a bike that was a few feet away. The bike had a bent wheel and several spokes torn loose. She stared at the bike for a few seconds and started to cry.

"Honey, what's wrong?"

"That's my bike. That bastard stole those bikes from Mom and the kids. I'm glad those people killed the lousy sons a bitches."

They ran for several hours without talking until Jo heard barking off to the side of the road. They were ready for a break, so she led Bill off the road, dropped her backpack, and picked up her AR. She walked into the woods with Bill right behind her. They only made it a few feet when she saw a large German Shepard sitting by a brush pile. He saw them, wagged his tail, and jumped up and down. He couldn't come to them because his leash was caught on a limb in the brush pile.

Jo slowly approached, and the dog licked her hand. She untangled the leash and unhooked it from the dog. He jumped up on his hind legs, placed his paws on her shoulder, and licked her face.

Bill poured some water into his cupped palm, and the dog lapped it up and begged for more. While Bill gave more water to the dog, Jo looked for something to pour water into for him. She found a large plastic drink cup, cut it down to about four inches tall, and gave it to Bill.

"I'll bet the poor thing hasn't had anything to eat for a couple of days. He was probably chasing a rabbit when his leash got caught on that limb."

Jo found a can of Spam in the stroller and cut a thick slice for the dog. He wolfed it down and whimpered for more. She fed the entire can full to him a slice at a time.

"His collar has a brass plate that says Max and a number to call if he gets lost. I'll bet his owner is somewhere dead out on this road."

"Well, he can catch rabbits now and get to the water. Our job is done. Let's get back on the road before we stiffen up," Bill added.

Max heard a noise in the brush and took off. He went crashing through the woods barking at whatever he was chasing. They went back onto the road and headed south again.

Jo looked over at Bill and said, "That felt good helping that dog. I hope a kind person helps our kids get home."

Jo and Bill took Highway 249 South out of Glasgow and ended the day covering 40 miles. They were only 20 miles as the crow flies from Bob's house. They had turned off Highway 249 onto Highway 261 and were going to camp in the woods when Bill noticed that over half of the houses appeared to be deserted.

This proved to be wrong. They checked the first three houses, and people shot at them. The fourth house was empty, and it had a large in-ground pool. A swim and a bath sounded great to Jo. They watched the place for over thirty minutes and then peeked into several windows before declaring the place empty. Jo tried the doors and found they were all locked; however, the guesthouse beside the pool was unlocked and was a small apartment with a bed and small kitchen.

They ate a quick meal, swam for an hour after dark, and then slipped into bed as tired as they were the night before. They were sound asleep when Jo woke up and heard a low growl outside the open window. She woke Bill, dressed, and grabbed her AR before peeking out the window. She could barely make out the German Shepard below the window. He growled a low growl again then lunged at a shadow barking as he ran.

Jo stepped outside with Bill at her heels. There were a flash and a gunshot. Jo shot one of the shadows and heard Max continue to growl.

"Get your fuckin' dog off me. Help, he's killing me!"

Jo turned her flashlight on to find Max had a man's arm in his mouth and was standing on the man's chest. She searched around and found another man in a prison jumpsuit dead on the ground.

"Why did you try to rob us?"

"This is my house. You were robbing me."

"So when did prison jumpsuits get so fashionable asshole?"

"Screw you bitch. Get this dog off me, and I'll show you who's an asshole. The man reached for his pistol with his free hand."

"Max, attack."

Max dropped the man's arm and bit down into his neck shaking the man like a rag doll. The man went limp as blood squirted from his neck.

"Max, heal."

Max walked over to Jo and sat at attention beside her right foot. He licked his lips and looked up at her as to say, "What's next boss. I killed the bad person."

"What just happened? The dog killed that man."

"Good boy. Good Max. Max must be a highly trained Police or security dog. He just kept that man from shooting one of us. Come on in Max. You can sleep in the house."

Max balked and laid down on the front porch. He started eating something, and Jo went to him to see what he was eating.

"Max caught that rabbit. We now have a guard dog. Let's go back to sleep. It's 3:00 am."

"Do you think it's safe?"

"I think we have a new watchdog. Go to sleep and Max will watch over us."

Jo lay still while Bill fell asleep. When she was sure he was asleep, she quietly dressed and walked out on the porch. There was a low growl, and then she heard Max's tail thumping the porch as his tail wagged. Jo sat down beside Max and stroked his back for a while before noticing the dead men off to the side. She dragged them around to the back of the guesthouse and left them to rot.

She then went to the back door. She picked the lock using two hairpins and was quickly inside the house. She didn't think of this as robbery since the house was abandoned at the end of the world. The house was very nice and obviously belonged to one of the richer people in the area. She searched for weapons, ammo, and food. She took several bottles of orange juice, canned meat, a loaf of bread, and a package of candy bars from the kitchen. She searched the master bedroom and was embarrassed by the sex toys in one of the nightstands.

She found a Ruger LCP .380 with a box of ammo in the other nightstand and tucked it into her waistband. She borrowed a pillowcase to hold her booty until she could store it in the stroller. She bypassed money, jewels, and other valuables since that would be stealing.

She locked the door and stored the booty in the stroller and her backpack except for a couple of cans of tuna, the loaf of bread and the orange juice. She went back to the guesthouse and woke Bill up with a kiss.

"Good morning husband."

"Good morning beautiful. I guess the guard dog kept us safe last night."

"Yes, and he has adopted us. We are his new forever family."

Bill dressed while Jo prepared their breakfast. She made a sandwich for breakfast and two for lunch. Bill sat down at the table and noticed the orange juice bottles.

"I will assume that I need to just drink the OJ and not ask too many questions."

"You are a smart man. Enjoy."

"Aren't you going to feed the dog?"

"No, he ate a rabbit last night, and I think he will forage for his food. We can't spare human food for pets anymore. Hell, we'll be damn lucky if we don't have to eat …"

"Girl, don't say that. I hope and pray to God that we don't have to do what I told you not to say."

Max looked up at Bill, cocked his head, and barked.

"See, he doesn't think dog stew is a good thing either."

They were on the road by 7:00 and headed south again. They were both tired but knew they had to keep ignoring their tired and aching muscles until they found their children.

Bill picked up the pace and started to leave Jo behind when he said, "Come on Jo kick it up a notch. We can be at Dad's house by noon if we speed up a bit."

"Bill, I'll try, but I'm exhausted."

Jo pictured her children in trouble and was able to increase her pace to match her husband's speed. The miles flew by until Bill pulled off the road and broke out the sandwiches.

"We've been running for two and a half hours. Let's eat a sandwich, pee, and get back on the road in 15 minutes."

"Hon, I can't wait to see Mom and the kids. I hate to think what they had to go through to get there safely," said Bill.

"I know your Dad told you that the first two to three days are the safest, and then it becomes more dangerous each day afterward. We will see millions of people leave the cities and search the countryside for food. That's when the situation will be the most dangerous."

"I never took Dad seriously about TEOTWAWKI. I actually thought he was a raving lunatic. I think I became a liberal just to piss him off. We have to do what it takes to help our family survive and then help others if possible. My family eats before all others. I won't feed anyone who won't work."

"Damn, Bill, you've become a conservative."

"Urgh."

"I know it hurts but get used to it. You'll make the final conversion when "The Walking Democrats" try to steal our food, rape, and plunder."

"Jo, that was uncalled for."

"The federal government has fed millions of these people for 60 years without most of them lifting a finger. Who is feeding them now? Riots, burning cities, and lawlessness are in full swing by now in the cities. Cities on fire must be avoided from now on."

"Time to hit the road."

They ran another two hours with Max trotting beside Jo before they saw the large cooling tower for the canceled nuclear power plant just outside of Dixon Springs. There was a sign on the right at the entrance to a large industrial complex that said there was a TVA station in the complex.

"Well we're only a few miles from Dad's place," Bill said in an excited voice.

"I know; I can't wait to see everyone."

A few minutes later Bill said, "Look, there is Higher's Drive. That's where we cut off to get to Rome Road and on to Dad's place."

They made the turn and saw a group of men standing in the Post Office parking lot. There were a half dozen armed men and a couple of women standing around the bed of an old pickup truck.

Bill waved as they approached and several of the men came out to meet them blocking their way.

"Where is you going? And who you be? You ain't from around these parts."

Bill replied, "We're heading to my father's house on down the road a piece. Now if you get out of the road we'll go on. We don't want any trouble."

One of the men raised his shotgun and started to point it at Bill. Jo drew her Glock, shot the man, and yelled, "Police. Drop your weapons or I'll shoot."

Another man whirled around as he raised his pistol, but Max jumped him and was tearing the man's arm to pieces when Jo called, "Max heal."

Max sat beside Jo but kept snarling at the men.

Jo said, "Move, and I'll drop all of you. I have 16 more bullets, and that's more than enough for a bunch of thugs like you."

"Do you think you can kill us all before we shoot you?"

Bill drew his Glock and said, "I'm going to shoot you first, and then we will kill every last one of you bastards. Drop your guns, or you die. One...two..."

Every man and woman dropped their guns.

"Now, Bill, throw their guns in the bed of the truck. I'll get in the back with Max and the stroller. I'll watch these fine people until we get a mile down the road. Then we'll park this piece of shit truck. If you try to follow, I'll shoot every one of you."

Bill lifted the stroller into the bed and then watched the people as Jo climbed into the bed. Jo waved bye as Bill sped off toward his Dad's place. He only drove half a mile before he saw a roadblock up ahead and slowed down.

"Give me the binoculars. Thanks."

Bill surveyed the two men at the roadblock and said, "That's Greg. He's one of Dad's friends. I'm going to drive up slowly. I'd holster the pistol."

Bill took off his white shirt and waved it out the window as they approached the roadblock. He parked the truck on the side of the road about 50 feet away and Jo, and he walked up to the men with their palms facing the men.

"Greg, is that you?'

"Yes, who are you?"

"I'm Bill. Bob Karr's son. This is Jo, my wife."

"Good to see you again. Bob has been as nervous as a cat in a room full of rocking chairs waiting for you to arrive. Was that Gunfire we heard coming from town?"

Bill replied, "Some of the townsfolk weren't happy to see us and tried to block our way. Two died for that mistake, and we kept their weapons and truck. We told them they could come down here and get them."

"I'll take care of the truck and weapons," the other man said.

Jo blurted out, "Have my Mom and our kids arrived."

"Yes, they came in last night.

"Are they okay?"

"Yes, but one of the girls has a flesh wound but is doing alright."

"Oh my God. We have to get to her now. My husband is a nurse."

"She's okay, but I know you want to get there fast so just drive the truck on down to Bob's place. We'll deal with it later. I'll call over the radio and get everyone back home."

It was only a few minutes later, and they were finally at Bob's house. Bill honked the truck's horn, and before they could get out of the truck, Bob and Jake were flying out of the house to greet them. There was a chorus of 'Mom and Dad' filling the air.

Then it was Jake asking, "Mom where did you get the dog? Can I play with him?"

"Jake, don't play with him unless I'm with you. He is a guard dog, and I don't know how he will react around kids."

As if to answer, Max walked over to Jake and lay at his feet. Jake patted Max, and they were friends.

They all hugged and then went in to see Missy who was awake and eating a late lunch.

"Darling, I'm so sorry that you had to go through this journey and encounter with those bad people."

"Dad, we ran over the leader with a tractor and shot several of the others. Those assholes should have minded their own business and left us alone. We can take care of ourselves."

Maddie, Will, and Jane drove up and ran over to see Jo and Bill.

"Hey, this is Maddie. We found Maddie on the road and kept her. She is one of us now."

Missy was in rapid fire mode, and no one else could get a word in edgewise. She finally wound down, and Bill checked her bandages and pronounced the patient was doing quite well.

Jo hugged her baby girl and said, "I'm very proud of all of you. If possible, your Dad and I need to get some of this dirt off and then we can sit down and swap stories about our trip down here."

Jane and Will hugged both Jo and Bill and sat down to join the conversation. Maddie sat beside Will and enjoyed the loving family.

Bill took a big gulp of warm beer and said, "Dad, I know you never thought that you would hear me say this, but you were right all along about being ready for TSHTF. I was very glad I remembered some of what you preached and I know I need to learn more. Civilization is gone and won't be coming back soon."

"Son, I knew it was coming, but I prayed it wouldn't. Your whole family did what it took to get the Hell out of Dodge and to safety. I'm very proud of all of you. Now the hard part starts."

"I know, Jo told me about "The Walking Democrats." Do you really think it will be that bad?"

"Son, what would you do to get food for your kids if they hadn't eaten in four days and hadn't had a decent meal in weeks?"

"The thugs, criminals, and assholes will become worse, and we just shoot them down like the rats they are, but what do we do with honest men and women who are just trying to feed their starving children."

"I guess we share our food."

"Son you arrived with two backpacks with two day's supply of food for two people. The good news is you are my family, and I prepared and will share with you assuming you will work in the fields to grow food and take up arms to defend our little group. You will also help earn your keep by supplying your nursing skills to the community. We can't share our food, or we won't be able to feed ourselves or our kids."

"Millions will die."

"Yep. But it's billions with a B. In 90 days, about 70% of the civilized world's population will be dead from starvation, murder, and disease. We can only save ourselves and can't worry about the others. We help when we can but not at our expense."

"It will be awhile before we're on the same page, but I'm catching up."

"Greg told me y'all had some trouble getting through town."

"Yes, some good old boys tried to block us from coming down this way. One pulled a gun, and Jo shot him and another asshole before they could shoot. I drew mine, and they became cowards and dropped their guns."

"Son, I hope you never have to kill a man. It stays with you forever."

"Dad, we ran into a bad bunch that had captured some women and were going to raid a family in a farmhouse. I killed three or four, and Jo killed as many. I didn't want to, but it had to be done to save the people's lives. Dad, this shit has made me reflect on my values. I still stand for taking care of people that need the help and believe in non-violence; however, I've seen firsthand that not everyone shares my beliefs. I will not let those bastards hurt my family or me. I won't feed them if it takes food out of my family's mouth."

"Son I am proud of you, but I am sad that everyone doesn't share your beliefs. There are too many people that are just plain lazy and want someone to give them life's necessities and others that are just plain evil. Sorry, you had to go through this, but it has just started."

"Yeah, Jo and I discussed it on the way down here. She calls the hordes of people leaving the cities "Walking Democrats.""

Bob gagged and spit his beer out on the porch, "That's my kind of woman."

"I know Dad, but she's mine, and I am coming much closer to her way of thinking. And yours."

Son, tomorrow after we have a big group hug I want to take you and Jo over to Greg's and have you two join our council. We are planning how to survive down here in the Horseshoe."

"Naturally, we'll be glad to pitch in and help any way possible."

"My thoughts are that you will take on health care and doctoring. We know there will be injuries and sickness, but I

154

want to get ahead of any issues that would spread disease. Then I want Jo to start our Police Force. Jack Fulkerson will concentrate on external attacks while Jo hands internal crime and any conflicts. We will all be soldiers if we are attacked. Jane will split duties between the hospital and security.

That reminds me that the kids will be trained how to handle guns and they will become part of our army. They also must start going on the scavenging trips and join in the work crews. These teens are the same age as my grandparents when they were married and had their own farm. Kids will become adults at 14-15 shortly."

"But Dad, they are so young."

"Son that I know. What would happen to Missy and Jake if the kind of thugs you had to kill ran over our settlement and took charge."

"I'd rather not think about it, but I get the point. We all live together or die together defending each other."

"Now you get it. Of course, we won't throw them into battle unless absolutely necessary, but they have to know how to fight and be prepared to fight. Another question is –what will this world look like in 10 to 20 years when the kids are grown? We need to teach them survival skills and give them as much education as possible to help rebuild our civilization."

"Damn, I need a shot to go with this beer."

Bill didn't hear his wife walk up behind him and his father during the conversation. She listened for a minute then left for their bedroom.

"Hon, are you asleep?"

"No, I was waiting for you to rub my legs so I could fall asleep. Those big strong hands feel so good on my thighs and calf muscles," Jo said as she flirted with her husband.

"I'll do yours if you do mine," he said as he started at her feet and worked his way up her legs."

Jo massaged Bill's legs as he talked, "Dad and I had a great conversation. I'll never be as conservative as you and Dad are, but I have to admit this adversity has made me reflect on how to keep my family safe from the very same people that I felt sorry for earlier this week."

"I am very proud of you, and I know that you will always have a soft spot for the downtrodden, but I am happy that you have learned that sometimes you have to make a stand against bad people. I wish this hadn't happened; however, I feel much better about our chance of survival now that you and Bob are teamed up to help protect our family."

"Dad made it a point to remind me that Missy and Will are almost adults in this new world and that teens will be working beside adults in the fields and on the battlefields."

"I've given that some thought also and I think our boy Will is interested in Maddie."

"She is a very intelligent and beautiful young lady. She could be your twin sister."

"Bill what I was getting to is we have them sleeping just a few feet away from each other."

"Jake and Missy are between them. Besides, if a girl and boy want to do some cuddling, they will find a way to do it."

"I know, but they are too young to raise a family."

"Jo, I love hearing you say you are proud of me."

"Keep rubbing my feet."

*

Chapter 10

Day Three – Alliance of Evil

"Sheriff the Kroger is on fire and looters have taken all of the food."

"What happened? I thought we nipped that in the bud by posting that we would shoot looters on sight," Replied the Sheriff.

"It's not our people. It's assholes from Nashville. Three old dump trucks brought in several loads of the looters before we could react. I don't know what to do."

The Senator answered, "Mable, round up all of the Deputies and ask Rich to deputize some of our rifle toting citizens to run this scum out of town. Buck tell our men to shoot to kill. I don't want a single looter to survive, and I want our food back. **Now**!"

The Sheriff and his Deputies left in a hurry and left the Senator watching them step on each other's feet as they scrambled to get away from the Senator. The Senator saw a movement out of the corner of his eye, looked up and saw a man in a police uniform walk into the station.

"Is there a fire or a robbery? Those clowns were sure in a hurry," the man said.

The Senator took offense then realized the man was right. This put a smile on his face, and he replied, "Your patch says Louisville Police Department. Aren't you a long way from home?"

"That I am. I left Louisville to get away from the drug addicts, looters, and gangs. It appears I didn't go far enough south."

"Perhaps those types need to be eliminated."

"That was always the case; however, those damned politicians always balked when the criminal's family sued the government."

"Sir, I'm Senator O'Berg, and I am the only authority in this county, and I say kill all criminals, thugs, gangs and looters."

"Well damn, that's my kind of law. Swear me in, and I'll get to work. I brought my own hardware. I hope my fully automatic M4's are okay to rid the town of this trash."

The Senator thought, *'what the heck. He'll either kill criminals or get killed'* and said, "Go to the Kroger store and tell the Sheriff I put you in charge of dealing with the criminals."

"Done. We need to talk about housing and pay later after the crooks are dead. Oh, I don't bury them; I just kill them."

"Put you gun where your mouth is, and we'll have a deal."

The Senator followed the man out the door; he hopped in an old pickup and headed to the store. The Senator waved at his assistant to fetch his car, and they followed the man to the Kroger store."

Walt walked up to the Sheriff with an M4 in his hand, another on his shoulder and two 9mm Berettas strapped to his tactical vest and said, "Tell your men to follow me and cover my back. Oh, the Senator placed me in charge of this turkey shoot."

"Now wait a minute. We can't go in guns a blazing. These folks deserve a trial."

The Senator yelled from behind the Sheriff, "Let the man do what I told you to do. Looters are shot on sight. Do any of you so-called Deputies want to join the Sheriff as he leaves town? If not do what this man says."

"I'm Walt Long, and we are going to kill every last one of these looters."

"What about the women and teens?"

"Looters are looters. Follow or get the fuck out of my way."

Walt marched towards the looters and started shooting as he moved using very carefully placed shots to drop a looter each time he fired. Several men were armed but were quickly killed by Walt or his six deputies. They killed over fifty of the scum in a few minutes, and then took half an hour to find the ones trying to hide.

When the killing was done, Walt walked over to the Senators 1959 Cadillac and said, "The trash has been dealt with. Do you have any other serious problems to take care of before I go to find me a place to live?"

"No. Walt that was a job well done. My administrative assistant will take you around town and find a home suiting my new Police Chief's needs. Be in my office at 10:00 in the morning, and we'll discuss salary and benefits."

The house was along the seventeenth fairway at Five Oaks and was a mansion compared to what Walt had lived in before. The admin lady left after telling him that a crew would deliver a few things that would make life better. The pool looked clear, so Walt went skinny dipping for an hour before taking a nap.

The crew arrived a few hours later with plenty of food, water, and alcohol. They also brought a generator to keep the refrigerator and lights in operation.

Walt sat back in his new recliner and thought, 'this is a nice place to stay until I find Jo.'

"They killed every looter. I ain't shitting you. They threw about sixty men, women, and kids into a dump truck and hauled them out of town to who knows where."

"Buck wouldn't do that. He's crooked, but he's not a killer."

"Jim, the Senator fired Buck and told him to leave town. This new man walked right into the middle of the looters and started shooting like he was invincible. He killed most of the looters by himself and the truth be told, he killed all of the kids. Our Deputies wouldn't shoot at the kids."

"Looters should be shot on sight but not kids. What else have you heard?"

"One of my son's friends is a Deputy. Walt Long, the new Police Chief told them that a big part of their job was going to be tax collection. The Senator will be posting a new decree that states everyone will give the county 20 percent of everything they manufacture, grow or produce in any form or fashion to support the government so they can protect us and keep the county operating."

Jim Dickerson thought for a moment and replied, "Hell, we'd be better off if the county government disbanded."

Jim went home and told Hoss about his conversation, and then they drove to all of his friend's houses on the west side of Lebanon and invited them to a meeting at his house.

Jim welcomed his visitors, and his wife served cookies and fresh milk during the meeting.

Jim started the meeting by filling everyone in on what the Deputy had passed on to Jim's city friend.

After he had finished bringing them up to date, Jim added, "It appears that we have ourselves a dictator who plans to rob us blind. He and his faithful followers can sit on their asses in the city and then take our food and possessions. Well, I for one won't go along with this plan."

"Jim I agree, but what can we do to stop them. They have the Sheriff and all of the Deputies on their side."

"We will warn them to stay in the damned city and leave us alone. If they come to steal our food and other stuff, we will shoot them like the criminals they have become. I'm going to town tomorrow to attend the Council meeting and make sure they know that we won't stand for this dictatorship."

Jim Dickerson and three of his neighbors drove into town to the City Hall and asked to speak with the Mayor.

"The Mayor left town right after the lights went out. Jim, I'll see if the Senator has time to meet with you."

Jim raised his voice and said, "I don't need the damned Senator. I want to speak to the new Mayor."

"Jim, now calm down. The Senator has taken charge of the city and county leadership."

"On whose authority? Did we have a vote and no one told us out in the county."

The Senator came out of the Mayor's office and said, "Why the raised voices. What's going on here?"

Jim walked up, looked O'Berg in the eye, and said, "There's a rumor that you run the Mayor off and have become a dictator. You have not been voted into leadership here and have no authority."

"Now Jim you know that I am the highest Federal Government Official and that puts me in charge."

"That's bullshit, and you know it. We will have a free election and decide who is in charge of our county and our city. It certainly isn't a crooked Senator from DC."

At that time, Walt and several Deputies rushed into the room with guns drawn.

The Senator barked, "Walt, tell your men to holster their guns. We need to resolve this peacefully."

Walt and his men holstered their weapons, but he said, "Senator these men have pistols. If they make a movement to draw them, we will shoot to kill."

Jim turned around to face Walt and said, "Who is this mouthy little bastard. I don't know who you are, but we elect Mayors and Sheriffs, and neither of you is in charge. We will hold an election ASAP and put duly elected officials in charge of this county, not a bunch of crooks and outside want to be policemen."

"Now Jim calm down. I am in charge, and if you try to stir things up, you are going to jail."

"Well you can try and put my men and me in jail, but you will have a hundred men from the county come in guns blazing to rid you vermin from this cesspool. Come on men, we have to let everyone in the county know about these dictators and hold a fair election."

162

Jim and his three men left and walked toward their truck.

"Senator, do you want me to put their sorry asses in jail?"

"The Senator looked over at the City Office Manager and said to Walt, "No. they're just blowing off steam and don't know how things work in politics. Come on into my office I need to see you about a traffic problem."

The Office Manager said, "Excuse me. Jim knows exactly what he is talking about. When the Mayor and Sherriff left, we should have had an election to replace them. I will get the ball rolling on that. We don't need to worry a man of your importance with local matters. You need to get back to Washington and help restart the country."

There was a round of applause from the group of public servants who had gathered in the common office area.

The Office Manager and three of the staff didn't come into work the next day. They were never seen again. The word spread around the city, and no city or county worker challenged the Senator again.

Jim sent the three men and his son out to round up all of the ranchers and farmers to attend a meeting at his home to discuss the situation. He warned them to tell everyone to come armed and to watch out for the new Police Chief and his henchmen.

Jim had to have the meeting in his barn since over 125 men, and women showed up for the meeting. Jim took charge and told the group what he knew.

"The Senator has taken control of our local government. The Mayor, Police Chief, City Manager and a handful of others have disappeared. O'Berg hired a thug named Walt Long as our new Police Chief, and he replaced Buck. The Senator has had these posters placed all over town and has kids on bicycles

163

posting them on telephone poles and hand delivering them to our houses. The memo poster says that there is now a 20% tax in effect. The fine print says that we have to give him 20 percent of all food, crops, guns, ammo, gas and all cars and trucks. The bastard is generous and says we can keep all farm equipment."

The majority of the people were furious at the play to take their possessions and food.

One woman spoke up and said, "Does that idiot know that we are all barely getting by and need the food to make it until our crops come in this fall."

Jim said, "The son of a bitch wants the food to feed the Police and government workers that are still on the job. I don't have a problem helping feed the police, firemen, and medical people, but he has put his own people in and is running the local government like a dictatorship. I won't put up with this."

"What do we do when the Senator sends these tax collectors out to steal our stuff?"

"Tell them to get off your property and if they don't shoot them."

Several men and women started walking out of the meeting, and one said, "We can't go shooting our policemen. I'm leaving before you get me involved in a war."

"Alonzo, you are in a fight to survive. These people are crooks standing behind a badge. None of our old Deputies have a badge anymore."

"I'm still not shooting at police."

Only 10 of the 125 left the meeting, and the rest spent the next hour starting their own community and government. They chose Paul Williams to be the County Mayor and Jim Dickerson to be the Sheriff. Jim asked Hoss and nine other men with police or military experience to become his Deputies.

"Senator, one of my Deputies, has a brother who attended the meeting out at Jim Dickerson's place. They have us outmanned three to one. It might be time to cut our losses and move on to easier pickings," said Walt.

"No my friend. We will cut the head off the snake, and the tail won't rattle long. Have your most trusted men find half a dozen motorcycles. I heard there is a terrible Motorcycle gang headed this way and they are a murderous bunch. I even heard they rape and kill farm women after they kill their men."

"That's why you get paid the big bucks. The country bumpkins will be begging for protection from the attacks, and they will be glad my men killed all of the bad guys. It's a shame that a few vocal assholes get killed by the gang before we run them off."

"Make sure the first target is a family that supports us and is vocal about supporting me. That will keep them off balance. Oh, make sure a kid or woman escapes to tell how bloody the carnage was and then burn them in their house."

"I ain't raping or abusing kids."

"Just slap them around a bit and kill most of the adults."

"I won't hurt young kids. Now teens that loot will get shot."

*

Chapter 11

Day Four – Family Reunion

Will woke up that morning wondering how his family would survive without hospitals, a federal government, TV, and cell phones. He was also nervous about how the adults had taken his suggestions. In retrospect, he thought he'd come on a bit strong. He sat up in bed leaning against the trailer's wall thinking about the past three days when Missy came up and sat down on the bed.

"Missy, you're supposed to stay in bed. Mom will beat you for getting out of bed before your arm is healed."

"Willie, it hurts, but I'm okay. I thought you were wonderful last night. You did what the rest of us were too afraid to do. They might be adults, but we have brains and can do most of what they do. Several of the other teens told me that they were afraid to speak up to the adults."

"Missy's right. I'm very proud of you also," said Maddie as she crawled onto the bed and sat beside Will.

"I just had to speak up. Maddie, you are 17, Missy is 15, and I'm almost 17. A hundred years ago, we'd all be married and have kids of our own. I know most people our age are more into video games and texting. Missy and I were raised in the outdoors. Papaw and Mom taught us a lot of skills that we can use now that the shit hit the fan. Maddie, I'll bet you are an outdoors person also."

"I kinda' like both worlds. I can be a girlie girl one day and hike the Appalachian Trail the next. What I want to quickly learn is how to handle guns, hunt, and fish."

"Willie can teach you those things. He helped me a bunch. Now I can shoot almost as good as he can."

"I'll be glad to teach you all I know. We also need to make sure that all of the teens and even younger kids get some survival training."

The trailer rocked slightly, and Jo entered closely followed by Bill.

"Hello, kids. We just wanted to see how you are doing this morning. We missed you so much, and I was afraid something bad would happen on the trip down. Missy, you should be in your bed."

"I had to chaperone these two besides, I feel much better if I don't move my arm too much."

Jake came running to his Mom and Dad and gave them hugs and kisses. Missy followed, and then Will pulled the covers around him and leaned over Maddie to kiss his Mom.

"Mom, we were worried about you and Dad. We both had trouble getting here, but our training saw us through. I'm now worried about the other people and especially the kids. The older people grew up on farms, but the kids have been spoiled. I know country kids know more than city kids, but most have been spoiled by electronics and machinery that does all of the work."

Jo looked at her son and the other kids and said, "Well then, we just have to figure out what skills they need and set up the training. Your Dad and I will count on you older kid...err...young adults to help with the training."

"Good catch Mom. I know that I'm not as mature as you are, but I don't think we should be treated as kids either."

"We agree with that, but you can't have your cake and eat it too. You will all be assigned chores and duties to perform just like the adults. It will take all of our efforts to survive."

Will spoke up, "Mom we also need teachers and schools for the younger kids. They need reading, writing, and math, but they also need life skills such as hunting, trapping, making soap, how to make a fire without matches. That kind of stuff."

"You are wise beyond your years. We will cut out the crap and indoctrination, and get the kids back to the basics and add in a dose of survival skills. We have a few adults that need that training also. Now, Grandma and Papaw have prepared a big family breakfast, and all of you need to get some clothes on, wash up, and head to the kitchen before we assign chores."

Missy spoke up and asked, "Mom, can we find some clothes to wear. We all washed the clothes we wore down here, but we only have one change each and Maddie doesn't have any extra."

"Maddie, I'll give you some of mine that I left down here at Christmas. May not be your style, but I think they will fit you. Missy we'll have to check with the other families to see if we can find clothes that fit you. Mom will have the same issue. She is smaller than Maddie and me. We may have to go scavenging for some clothes before they are all taken."

168

Maddie replied, "Thanks for the clothes. I'm starting to wonder if I should move on to my home in Lebanon. Y'all only have so much food and supplies. You don't need another mouth to feed."

Jo leaned over to her, wrapped her arms around the girl, and said, "Maddie, you saved my babies from those robbers. We owe you, and we all want you to stay with us and become part of our family. Will always wanted an older sister."

"Mom!" Will said in embarrassment. His thoughts about Maddie were not the kind one has about your sister."

Missy and Maddie went into Maddie's room at the end of the trailer to get dressed. Jake and Will pulled the pocket door to the bunkroom and did the same.

"Maddie, I think Will likes you."

"I hope he does. I'm now his big sister according to your Mom."

"Maddie he doesn't need a big sister. Will needs a girlfriend, and I think you are his new girlfriend."

"I like Will, but this would be awkward to have my boyfriend sleeping in the same little trailer."

"I know, boys fart a lot."

"Well that, but I mean we share the same common area and bathrooms. It's hard not to be half naked some of the time. Your Mom and Dad wouldn't like that."

"Do you mean the way Mom stared at those black panties and half t-shirt you had on this morning while sitting beside your new boyfriend."

Maddie threw a pillow at Missy and Missy returned a middle finger.

"Maddie, Will's eyes were bugging out when you sat down beside him. When Mom came in, he looked at her or the wall and didn't look at you at all. Mom will give you some Granny clothes after breakfast."

Bob waited until everyone was seated around the table, and then he said the Lord's Prayer.

When everyone thought he was done, he added, "Lord thank you for bringing my family and our new family member home safely. Maddie may be the newest member, but she is now officially one of us. Now let's be thankful that we have something to eat and the skill to survive thanks to God. Amen."

They had fried eggs, rabbit, and biscuits for breakfast along with fresh milk and a steaming pot of coffee. They ate their fill, and then everyone pitched in to clean up and wash the dishes except Bob, Maddie, and Will who went to feed the horses and chickens.

Maddie went off by herself to feed the chickens while Bob and his Grandson tended to the horses.

"Will, that Maddie is a very nice young lady and she is a pretty filly to boot. I'll bet you haven't noticed though you being such a serious young lad."

"Papaw, I really like her, but I'm afraid that she likes me like a brother and not a boyfriend."

"Well son It's best to find out now instead of wondering, and she gives up on you and finds someone who does show interest in her. Ask her to go on a walk down to the river or take a horseback ride around the Horseshoe with her. Just stay away from the top of the Horseshoe."

"I know you're right. I just have to work up the courage."

"You'll do okay son."

They finished feeding the animals and walked back up to the house when Bob said to Maddie, "Will was just asking me if I thought you'd like to walk over to the river this evening. It's really pretty this time of year with the Dogwoods and Redbuds blooming along the bank. I told him, of course, you would."

"Will I'd love to walk to the river with you."

"Great, we'll head out once we get our chores done after supper."

They walked into the house and saw everyone was seated around the table. They took their seats, and Bob started the first family meeting.

"Jo in addition to being on the security team with Jane, I need you and Jane to take on additional duties. I want you two to take ownership of training the teens in survival skills. I suggest you use Maddie, Will, and Missy to help with the classes. I believe Betty Lou told me there are 21 young people between the age of 12 and 17 in the Horseshoe now that the last families have moved in to stay. They need everything from gun safety to how to skin a deer.

I also want you two to lead at least two scavenging trips this week and next week. That will give us a total of ten trips. As you would think the useable goods will taper off dramatically over the next two weeks."

"Bill, you will have your hands full setting up our little hospital and taking care of sick and injured people; however, I need you to also teach a First Aid Class a couple of times a week until everyone above ten years old has been trained."

"Dad, do we have any books or training supplies?"

"Yes, I have several good First Aid manuals and a couple of Army field manuals on First Aid."

Will, I also want you to do double duty helping with the fence building. Starting tomorrow, we will be working from sun

171

up to sundown. I want y'all to get settled in today and only work half a day.

Jo called Maddie to her bedroom and showed her some clothes that were lying on the bed.

"Pick out one outfit that you like plus a pair of my jeans. I think I'm a bit larger in the waist, but you're a bit bigger in the bust size. There are a bra and panties that should also fit One of our scavenging trips will focus on finding some clothes that fit all of us. Bill is lucky because all of his Dad's clothes fit him and are only a size too big for Will. Us ladies will need to do some serious shopping."

"Thanks so much for taking care of me. It's helping me to have you with me since I lost my mom," Maddie said as tears rolled down her face.

Jo sat down beside her on the bed and consoled her for a while until the tears stopped and Maddie said, "I have to stop blubbering and move on with my life. I'll miss Mom, but I have to be strong and not a burden to you or your family."

Jo corrected her, "It's now your family also. You are now a part of us."

Bob caught Will before lunch and took him to his garage. He opened a large gun safe and handed Will a Springfield M&P15 and a Ruger P95 9mm with a holster.

"Will grab that tactical vest hanging on the wall. It served me well many times, and I want you to have it. There are three 30 round AR Mags and three Magazines for the Ruger. Here are a bayonet and a .380 Keltek for a backup pistol. Use the leg holster and wear long pants anytime you are on guard duty. Always expect trouble. Take these boots too. They're about a half size too big, but you can wear double socks if needed.

You are a man now living in a dangerous world. Keep your weapons within arm's reach at all times. I'll outfit Missy and Maddie later this afternoon, but I expect you to watch over them and keep them out of trouble.

Anyone can pull a trigger and kill a punk. It takes a good man to know when to kill and when to retreat and live to fight another day. I'll give you my opinions, but you have a good head on your shoulders and will do well."

"Thanks, Papaw. I needed better weapons and won't let you or the others down."

"Now all I want in return is for you to live a long and bountiful life and you and your wife give me some great grandkids to mow my grass and tend the horses."

"Papaw. I don't even have a girlfriend."

"Maddie is one hell of a woman and beautiful to boot."

"I don't know if she even likes me."

"Trust me, she does."

Bob and Will went to join the fence building crew after lunch and Bob introduced him to the team. The leader gave Will a pair of gloves and a posthole digger and showed him where to dig the next ten holes. Bob went on to the road to see how the construction of the gate and guardhouse was going.

"Bob, I'll bet you are happy to see all of your family back under your roof," said Greg."

"Yes, it allows me to stop worrying and lets me focus on what we need to accomplish. We also gained a Policewoman, a Nurse and three young adults who can contribute labor, survival skills, and brain power."

"I was impressed with your Grandson, Will. He has a lot on the ball. How old is he?"

"He's 16 and will be 17 in June. He's very mature for his age, and I have had him down here for a month every year and taught him about survival, hunting, fishing and a thousand other things. I need to teach him more about how to court a young lady."

"I figured that he and Maddie would hook up eventually. He'd better move fast there are half a dozen men and boys interested in that young lady," replied Greg.

"I think he'll seal the deal this evening."

There was a commotion behind them, and they turned to see the guard arguing with three men.

"I asked you what you want, and until you tell me, I'm not getting anyone to talk to you."

"Screw you. Get Bob Karr over here right now."

Bob walked over to the gate and said, "I'm Bob Karr and why are you so rough on Izzy?"

"We know you stole all of the food from all of those trucks and we want our share."

"What make you think you deserve a share of anything we have?"

"Because we need it to survive and you have more than you need."

"Do y'all have plenty of seeds to plant in your gardens?"

"No. We're not farmers."

"Then how do you expect to live when your food runs out?"

"We'll get our share of your crops and the other farmers around the area."

"So you're willing to help plant, tend, and harvest the crops?"

174

"Hell no. We been on welfare for our whole lives. You rich people got to feed us."

"Where are you from? I don't think I know you. Greg do you know any of these men?"

"Never seen them before."

"We're from Nashville, and if you don't give us food, we'll take it," the man said as his hand went for his pistol.

Bob beat him to the draw, shot the man, and turned to see a pistol aimed at his chest. Before the man could pull the trigger, there was the sound of two shots and both of the remaining men confronting Bob dropped with holes in their chests. Bob turned to see who had saved his life and saw Will about 75 yards away with his AR in his hands running toward the gate. Greg was standing there dumbfounded that he didn't get a shot off before the three men were dead.

There was the sound of gunfire from up the road and bullets struck the gate and the unfinished guardhouse wall. Will dropped to his knee, steadied his rifle against a post, and returned fire along with the guard. Three men took off out from behind a tree and were running back toward town.

Will shot three times and two of the men dropped to the ground, and the third kept running.

Will walked over to his Papaw and said, "Papaw, are you alright. I saw that asshole go for his gun and had to drop the posthole digger and grab my rifle to shoot the other two. Damn, if I had a scope I could have shot the one that escaped."

"Bob, get the man a scope for that rifle. Boy, you saved our lives. That scum was going to rush the gate and take what they wanted. The five of them could have killed us."

"Papaw there's another two dead in the weeds where the men were hiding."

Bob, Will, and Greg walked out to the hiding spot and saw the two bodies. Sure enough, Will had killed one and wounded the other.

Bob yanked the man up by his shirt and said, "Why did you come here. Who told you about this place?'

"The sign up on Highway 25," was all the man had said before he died.

Bob yelled over to Izzy, "Izzy, please go get a dump truck and a couple of men with long guns. We're going to town, and we need to be ready for a fight."

Izzy drove the dump truck with Greg in the passenger's seat and Bob, Will and the two extra men in the bed of the truck. They all had ARs and shotguns. The dump bed was like having an armored vehicle. That is except for the driver and passenger.

They drove past the Post Office and on to Highway 25, and as the man said, there was a big sign that said,

Food this way →

Rich People Won't Share.

Bob and Will jumped down from the truck, tore the sign down, and then Bob set it on fire. While they watched it burn several men with dirty clothes walked up and watched. One poked the other one and laughed.

Bob held his AR in front of him and said, "I don't know why six men dying because they tried to steal our food is funny. I will personally hunt down and kill the son of a bitch that puts another sign like this up. Do you two scumbags hear me?"

The men were high on something and could only laugh and mumble their words.

Then Bob noticed that there was a group of people walking toward the dump truck. They were pushing grocery carts, wheelbarrows, and handcarts. It looked like something from a third world country.

One of the men walked toward Bob and asked, "Mister, do you have any food that you can spare?"

I'm sorry; we barely have enough to feed ourselves. Try Carthage on down Highway 25."

"Are there any empty houses that we can live in around here? We need a place to stay. There wasn't any food in Cincinnati or Louisville."

"Sir, I don't think you understand. There isn't any extra food here either. Keep walking south."

"We have cash. We can pay for food."

"Money is worthless since the lights went out. Keep heading south."

A woman from the group walked over and said, "So you will let my three kids starve instead of helping us."

"Woman, if I give you my kid's food then they will starve. I'm not going to let my kids starve because you need food. Not get your asses out of here before I lose my temper."

The group walked away after shouting a few obscenities at Bob. Greg, Izzy, and Will joined Bob as they watched small groups of people walk by them. Most of the people were dirty, and there was no gleam in their eyes. They just kept putting one foot in front of the other and walked down Highway 25 toward Carthage. Only a few were heading north.

Greg mentioned, "Do y'all think we need to place guards up here to keep people from coming down the road to the Horseshoe?"

Will pointed behind them toward the Horseshoe and said, "Those people came down Dixon Springs Circle Road and came out behind us. We need a checkpoint south of the junction. I'd also post some Dead End signs up and maybe some Biohazard signs. Thousands of people will be coming down this road for the next few weeks. As time goes by they will get more desperate and dangerous."

Greg replied, "I'll go house to house and let the ones living between us and the roadblock that they are free to come and go, and that we are just trying to stop the hordes from getting down our road."

"I'll get a crew to bring up some barricades and stage some dead cars for cover," replied Bob.

Will added, "We have an unlimited supply of water in the Horseshoe. Let's place some drums of water by the checkpoint and let them fill their bottles. Then we can pump them for news about the rest of the country or maybe find some decent people with skills we need and get them to join our community."

"Both are damn good ideas. Get er done," replied Bob.

Will helped Bob and Greg set up the checkpoint and then hauled water up from the closest well to fill the two 50 gallon drums. He was busy working when his Papaw walked up and said, "Will don't you have something to do this evening?"

"Oh, yes, I do. I'm going to take the ATV and head back to your house and get cleaned up before supper."

Will snuck into the trailer and took a bath the best he could with cold water and a washrag. He looked in the mirror and saw a wind-burned face with a four-day growth of stubble. He looked for a razor and couldn't find one, so he snuck in the house and borrowed his Papaw's razor and shaving cream. Now he was clean and clean-shaven.

He went to the kitchen to see if he could help set the table and saw his Grandma and Mom preparing dinner while Missy was lying on the couch resting. He asked his Mom if he could help with anything and she told him, "Go watch TV until supper."

"Mom, you told me to go watch TV."

"Darn, I guess you can read one of Papaw's old hunting magazines."

He looked around, didn't see Maddie anywhere, and sat down beside Missy.

Missy whispered, "Maddie is in Mom's room getting dressed up for your date."

Will threw a pillow at Missy, and then acted as though he was reading one of the magazines. A few minutes later Maddie came out of the bedroom, said hi and went on into the kitchen to help the other women. Will thought she was beautiful; he had only seen her with a dirty face and hair stuffed under a ball cap since he met her a few days back.

Bob and Bill arrived a few minutes before time to eat and quickly cleaned up for supper. As usual, Bob said grace, and then they ate. The conversation was lively since so much had transpired since the morning and everyone wanted to hear any news. There were no TV or radio newscasts, so things were sliding back in time to the time before newspapers and the five o'clock news. Most news was now passed on at the supper table or across the back of a pickup bed.

Bob interrupted the conversation to say, "I guess Will filled you in on how he saved my life this morning and kept several others of our group from being ambushed."

Jo and Bill both replied, "What happened?"

Bob filled them in on the events at the gate and ended by saying, "Jo and Bill, you have raised one hell of a young man. He shot the two that were about to kill me and then picked off two more over a hundred yards away that were shooting at the work crew. Will you are my hero."

Jane listened and said, "Well I'm not surprised at all. Will was a major factor in getting us down here safely. Son, you have grown into a man right in front of our eyes. I am very proud of you."

Bill and Jane hugged their son and were very proud but concerned parents. No 16 year old should have to kill to survive. It was a new world, and everyone would have to adapt or die.

They finished eating, and Jo went over to her son and said, "You and Maddie are excused from cleaning up. Have a good time."

Will went over to Maddie in the living room and said, "Maddie will you come with me for a walk."

They walked out the back door and cut across the fields to the river. Maddie and Will were silent for a few minutes, and then Will said, "Maddie this is the first time I've seen you without a baseball cap or a dirty face. You took my breath away when I saw you before supper."

Maddie just giggled and took Will's hand as they walked on toward the river. They chatted about their recent journey then talked about how dating would change now that there were no movies, malls or teen clubs. Will then told her about the history of the Horseshoe and the early settlers. Before they knew it, they were close to the river.

There was a spot south of Bob's house where the land was higher than the surrounding terrain. Also, a rocky cliff was perfect to jump off into the deep water below. There was also a tree close enough to have a rope to swing out over the water.

"The water is a bit cold now, but in a few weeks, it will be warm enough to swim comfortably. We came here most days and swam or fished most of the day. Papaw has a couple of canoes, and we would go all up and down the river. See the beautiful Redbuds and Dogwoods blooming in the woods."

"Will do you have a girlfriend?"

"No, but I did have one a few months back. She decided I was too boring. I don't like going to clubs or parties where the kids get drunk and do drugs. I like fun but nothing like that."

"Me neither. I guess we're both squares."

"See that tree over there."

"The one with the fork sticking up?"

"Yes, the sun always sets in the middle of the fork. We have about two hours before it sets."

"That's plenty of time to swim and get dry before going back home."

"We didn't bring swimsuits," Will replied."

"We don't need them."

Will's face turned red, and he got a big smile on his face.

"Get that goofy look off your face there won't be any skinny dipping until I get to know you better. We can swim in our underwear. Mine covers more than my Bikini. Come on let's swim."

"It will be cold."

"Chicken."

Maddie took her socks and shoes off then pulled her t-shirt over her head and laid it on a rock. Will stripped down to his briefs while she took her jeans off.

"Will, are you sure there are no rocks below that will kill us when we dive in."

"Sorry, I should have mentioned that we need to climb down the left side and walk into the water and make sure there are no sunken logs. The water is a bit murky to see very far into it."

He had tried to keep looking away from her as he followed her down the rocks to the water but caught himself sneaking peeks at her. When she got to the bottom, she turned abruptly, and he bumped into her. She put her arms around him, he drew her close, and they kissed.

"She looked into his eyes and said, "I was wondering when you would kiss me."

Will kissed her again for a longer time and then said, "I won't wait so long for the next one.

"Will, I like you but don't get greedy"

"I like you too."

"Come on; let's get in the water before it gets too hot up here."

Will spun around and walked into the water. She followed him in and went under the water.

"Oh shit. This water is cold," Maddie said.

Will swam around her testing for logs and then went under the water, and then surfacing directly behind her. He put his arms around her and drew her close. He kicked his feet to keep them above water, and she relaxed in his arms.

"You feel so warm, and the water feels so good. I haven't been this relaxed in days."

Will replied, "Reminds me of a country song about holding your body against me."

She replied, "Hold me close and never let me go."

They climbed back up the rock stairs and jumped into the water several times until they were exhausted. Will spread his clothes out on a large flat rock and they lay under the waning sun beside each other. Will tried several times to steal a kiss, but she turned her head each time.

"I thought you liked me, "said Will.

"I do, but you are moving too fast."

"Look the sun is above the fork in the tree," Will said.

"Forget the sun and kiss me."

"I thought I was moving too fast."

"You are. I like to call the shots."

"Some people would call that controlling or bossy."

"Not if they want to kiss me. Shut up and kiss me."

*

Chapter 12

Day Five – Family Surviving

The person walked along the edge of the field in the moonlight and kept in the shadows to avoid drawing any attention. There was dew on the ground and mist in the early morning air as the dark-clad figure headed towards the river. This was a scouting trip to determine if there was a way to get across the river in and out of the Horse Shoe.

The east side of the Horse Shoe would be surveilled before daybreak; the shadowy figure would go home and then search the west side the next night. Sneaking in and out of the house was easy since everyone was always tired these days and only one guard was posted. Avoiding the guard was not difficult, and after the local trash had been taken out, the black-clad figure would lobby for more security for the compound but not yet.

There was a noise up ahead, and it came from two men in a Jon boat. They rowed silently across the river from the far bank and talked as they paddled.

"Bo, I heard these folks have a shit load of food, guns and medical supplies."

"Yes, I was in the first meeting when they made plans and started robbing the hardware and gas station. They kept everything for themselves and told us tough shit."

"We can rob that barn a couple of times if we are careful."

They reached the shore, and the man in the front of the boat stepped out and pulled the boat up onto the ground.

"Jerry, I have to see a tree," the man said as he stepped into the shadows to relieve himself."

The figure dressed in black slipped up behind him with a knife, grabbed him from behind and cut his throat before he could make a sound. The Wraith let him fall to the ground and waited for the other man to search for his friend.

"Jerry. Where are you, Jerry? This ain't funny. Come on out from behind that tree. If you try to scare me, I'll shoot your sorry ass."

Bo carefully walked into the darkness and didn't hear the person slip up behind him. He pulled the trigger on the Glock 21 just as his jugular vein was severed. The report was very loud, so the Wraith quickly dragged both bodies to the river, placed a note in both men's pocket that just said, 'The Wraith," and pushed them away from the shore. The boat was a good find that night and was hidden in the bushes several hundred feet downstream. The boat would come in handy later to help take out the trash.

The black-clad figure walked quietly down the hall and into the room. Making almost no noise, the person undressed, got in bed with a big smile and went to sleep. It was only 3:00 am

185

and the first night was a success. There would be many more nights, and many more vermin were sent to meet their maker. All went to Hell.

Will woke up earlier than usual and had to use the bathroom, so he quietly walked through the living room to the bathroom. When he finished, he opened the door and was surprised to see Maddie looking at him.

She shoved him back into the tiny bathroom and shushed him to be quiet. She grabbed his face, kissed him on the forehead, and then she then said; "Now that's your good morning kiss. Now get out."

Will started to go when Maddie said, "Oh, I saw someone slipping into the house a few minutes ago. Does Bob have a secret girlfriend? Now go."

Will snuck back down to his end of the trailer, got dressed, grabbed his guns, and headed over to the house. The sun hadn't even thought about coming up, but a mixture of adrenaline and testosterone had Will keyed up and ready to go.

He quietly walked into the house and used his small flashlight to maneuver around the house to see who might have had company. He saw wet footprints leading to his Grandma's room. There was a faint light coming from under the door. He thought *who would be sneaking into Granny's room.* He scratched his head and walked into the kitchen.

Will fumbled around the kitchen in the dark and found the coffee and the coffee pot. He started a pot of coffee and grabbed a left over biscuit to chew on while the coffee perked. The sound of the coffee perking in the old steel pot on the Coleman stove sounded reassuring to him because that was the first thing his Papaw did every morning when they were camping.

"Son, you're up early this morning," said Bob.

"Good morning Papaw. It's a glorious day. I'm ready to get to work building the Great Wall of Jack."

"Now that's funny. How did your date go?"

"Great. She told me she likes me and we kissed a few times."

"That's great. She'll be your steady girlfriend soon. Now, son, I know that at your age your hormones are raging, but don't do anything that can't be undone."

"Papaw, are you going to give me the sex talk."

"Hell no! I hope your Dad did that years ago. I'm just the guy to remind you to not do anything that would be causing you to change diapers for the next several years."

"Mom gave me the talk; Dad's not good at that stuff. Wait until your Mom tells you about reproductive organs, proper use of rubbers, and being a gentleman."

"Whoa, I'm too old to be learning that stuff. Seriously, I know that you know the mechanics of sex. Just don't knock her up until we have a real doctor around here."

"Dad, that was not what a mother wants to hear her father in law telling her young son," said Jo as she entered the room.

"Then stop sneaking up on men when they're talking about women. You could get an embarrassing ear full."

"I heard enough of that crap around the locker rooms and bars with my Police friends. I apologize for listening to your conversation and will try not to do it again; however, I do agree with pop. Don't knock her up."

Jane rounded the corner and said, "Who are y'all not going to knock up? Will have you been bad?"

"Oh shit. Now both of my Grandparents and Mom are discussing if I got laid last night. We only kissed, and I don't even think she likes me."

The screen door banged and everyone shut up at the same time as Maddie and Missy walked into the kitchen. Missy looked from one to the other and said, "Y'all are talking about us; aren't you? Maddie, they shut up when we walked into the room."

Bob quickly replied, "No Jo hit her finger on the sink and said the F word.

Later that morning, Will saw his Grandma in the backyard tending to the garden.

"Grandma, I don't know how to say this err..."

"Just spit it out, boy."

"Do you have a boyfriend?"

"What, no and what brought up that question?"

"Well you jumped in on Papaw and Mom picking on me this morning about my love life, and Maddie saw a person dressed in black slip into the house early this morning. The grass was wet with dew, and I followed footprints to your bedroom door. I thought that you might be calling the kettle black."

"Shit, Will I went for a walk this morning when I couldn't sleep. Don't tell anyone because your Grandfather thinks all us women need to be protected. I can take care of myself. Wait a minute. I'm a grown woman and can slip around and err... visit men if I want to. I didn't but I can if I ever find one. You worry about your love life and don't worry about your Grandma's love life."

Will turned red in the face and said, "Grandma, I'm sorry if I offended you or embarrassed you."

"And I'm sorry for jumping your ass. Let's just say we're back to normal and I won't tease you about getting laid, and you won't mention my nightly forays."

"Okay," Will said, and then thought *nightly means more than once.*

Will caught Maddie and they took one of the ATV's up to the wall so Will could join the crew and Maddie could be trained to be a guard. They chatted during the short trip to the wall and Will filled her in on his conversation with his Grandma. Will also told her about being told not to get Maddie pregnant.

"So the Karr family just talks about me like I'm some kind of tramp trying to steal their baby boy," Maddie said.

"No, it was mainly Papaw teasing me. Please don't take offense. Papaw just wanted me to be cautious and not ...."

"Get me pregnant."

"Well yes. I politely told him to mind his own business."

"Did you tell him that you can't get pregnant from kissing? Besides you are too young for me and not my type at all."

"No. I was tongue tied and trying to get out of the conversation when the others walked into the room. I'm only a few months younger and what is your type?"

"So they think we did it yesterday down by the river."

"No, I told them we just kissed. I would never discuss anything we do with anyone. Well except kissing."

"Will I was just teasing you. Look I like you and like being with you, but you are not boyfriend material. I want an older more mature man in my life. Besides you might end up to be a wimp like your dad."

"Well I...."

189

"Hold on, I'm still talking. I also want to say that you have been a gentleman. Any other boy would have tried to feel me up while we were lying on the rocks."

"So I should have grabbed a feel, and you would like me more."

"No, I would have broken your fingers."

"You are crazy. Do you have any idea what you really want?"

"Hey, before you drop me off. The person dressed in black that I saw sneaking into the house had an AR on her shoulder and a mask over her face. I saw her silhouetted by the porch light. Looked more like a Ninja warrior than a grandma to me."

Will drove off mad, dazed, and confused. His heart was broken.

The fence was up, and the guard shack and gate were complete. Now the crew switched to building the wall by driving steel poles and roadside barrier metal into the ground and then bolting more metal barrier to the uprights. The wall would be six feet high and a thousand yards long. The wall was fifty feet south of the fence, had one emergency opening on the east side, and would have a chute up to the guardhouse and gate at the road. Two guard towers were placed about 250 yards from the riverbank on each side of the Horseshoe.

There were two crews working from the opposite riverbanks pounding steel uprights into the soft earth and two more bolting on the barrier rails. The work progressed quickly, and by noon, over three hundred total feet of the wall had been installed.

Will's team took a thirty-minute break for lunch, and he drove the ATV over to the gate to have lunch with his Papaw. He drove up to the gate and saw Izzie instructing Maddie and several other young adults. Izzie saw Will and waved at him. Izzie said, "It must be lunch time. Be back in thirty minutes."

Maddie walked over to where Will was sitting and joined him. Bob saw Maddie sit down beside Will and quietly went over to eat with Jack and the crew. Maddie and Will ate their sandwiches without speaking for several minutes.

"Will, I'm going to try to get Jane to talk Bob into sending out a scavenging team to find some women's clothes and hygiene products. You men don't want to have stinky women in the camp. We also need to stock up on TP. I'll be dammed if I'm using a corn cob or leaves."

"Why should I care if you stink? I'm not your type."

"Will I didn't want to hurt your feelings. I like you and want you as my friend. I'm sorry if I hurt you."

"Look, I like you also and that hurt. I guess I like you more than you like me. I'll be your friend and move on to find a girlfriend.

Back to what you said, as much as Grampa and I talked about an upcoming apocalypse, I never thought about feminine hygiene or toilet paper. I guess it's easy to take that stuff for granted."

"I guess it's easy to forget until you get Poison Ivy on your balls or your period starts. Men think about food, beer, guns, and ammunition."

"Don't forget beautiful girls named Maddie," replied Will as he said goodbye and went back to work.

Will's face was red, and he hurt down deep. He had fallen for Maddie, and she only wanted a friend.

The crew worked until the sun was hiding behind the trees that evening and Will was dead tired when he drove up in the ATV to pick Maddie and Bob up.

Bob climbed into the back seat and said, "Maddie, do you know where I can find a slightly older edition of you. It gets lonely, and I think I'm getting jealous of Will."

"I'm surprised that you and Jane haven't hooked up. She's witty, charming, and beautiful. You two would make a great couple."

"Funny that you should say that. I asked her if she was interested in seeing me the other day and she didn't say no, but neither did she say yes. We like each other, and I have been interested in her for a while, but she doesn't seem to care much for me."

Bob sniffed under his armpit and added, "Perhaps a bath every now and then would change her mind."

"Bob that would be a great start. You might also take her for a walk to the swimming hole. I understand it's a very romantic place to court a lady. The sun going down is beautiful."

"I'll give that a try. I think at times I need to be a bit more romantic and not so much of a tease."

"Yes on the romance but I find the teasing to be very attractive. If I were a couple of years older, I'd dump Will's ass and let you chase me until I caught you.

I just had a thought. I saw you talking with Mary this morning when she brought water around. You need to have Jane see you flirting with her. That will get her motor started."

"I'm not good at the romance game."

"Practice. I'll give you some tips."

Will walked with Maddie to the trailer and said, "You said that you'd dump me for Papaw."

"I was just kidding."

"What I'm getting at is to dump me we have to be going together."

"Boys sure are dumb. I was just joking."

"I was going to ask you to be my girlfriend tonight."

"Well, I'm sorry. I want to be your friend, just not a steady girlfriend."

Jo fed Jake but held supper until everyone came home from the hospital and work crews. Even Bill was dead on his feet from tending to patients with everything from a broken wrist to sunburns. There wasn't much conversation going around the table when Maddie said, "That widow woman, Mary, is real nice. She brought fresh water around three times today.

Will, she kinda hung around your Papaw a lot. Bob, you'd better watch out. I think she has designs on you."

Will caught on and added, "Papaw, a man once told me to be careful not to do anything that couldn't be undone. That's probably good advice for you also. Yep, she was making eyes at Papaw."

Bob smiled and replied, "I'm not saying she flirts with me, but I'm invited to her house for dinner on Sunday after church. Anything else is nun ya biznez."

Will kept an eye on his Grandma, and she definitely reacted to the story. Her face turned red, and she started fidgeting with her meal.

Maddie caught Jane after supper and Maddie said, "Jane, we need to set up a scavenging trip to focus on women's clothes, feminine hygiene products, and toilet paper. We need to find

193

some of the same for the men. Bob's interest in Mary reminded me that Will needs some aftershave or cologne."

Jane responded, "I've been thinking the same thing. I'll get permission from Bob and Jack. Don't worry about Romeo Bob. I'll pick something out just for him."

"You do that, but I wouldn't wait until Mary shares her dessert with him after dinner."

Maddie almost choked when Jane replied.

"I get your meaning, and Bob's only getting dessert at my kitchen table," Jane said as she walked to the back porch where Bob was sitting.

Jane joined Bob and soon had a glass of whiskey in her hand. They were laughing and swapping stories when Maddie and Will walked out to the gazebo by the garden and watched the moonrise.

"Will, what do you think happened?"

"I don't know. Perhaps the Iranians set off some EMP blasts above the USA. We might never know. I just hope we don't get invaded by another country like Russia or China. It's been five days, and we haven't seen a single airplane. I can't believe any country destroyed our entire military and government."

"It's like a science fiction movie where everyone in the government just disappeared," replied Maddie.

"I asked Papaw, and he said that he has two working radios and he isn't getting anything from the emergency channels. He said the short wave has several people talking every day, but they are just surviving like us and haven't heard from the government either."

"That's enough gloom and doom. Let's talk about something fun. That's what we need around here is something that's fun."

Will just sat there, listened to Maddie, and sulked.

*

Chapter 13

Day Six – The Wraith

The Wraith retrieved the black shirt, pants, hat, and mask from a trash bag under the bed and quickly got dressed. The Wraith strapped on the pistol belt and checked the pistol and knife to make sure they were secure. The sneakers had been white but had been turned black with a marking pen.

It was cloudy, and with no moon, it was very dark outside. The guard was patrolling the barn behind the house, so it was easy to slip out the front door and use the house to conceal movement from the guard.

This excursion was to take the Jon boat across the river and scout out the west side. The night was cold, and it was misting rain as the boat glided across the river. The only sounds were the crickets, tree frogs and an occasional owl hooting. The

Wraith was careful to keep sound to a minimum as the oar was stroked through the water. The bank of the river came into view, and the Wraith quietly pulled the boat up into the tall grass so it would be hidden from prying eyes.

Staying inside the tree line made the walk more difficult; however, not being caught was much more important. There were a dozen houses along this side of the river, and there were no lights until a red dot appeared up ahead. Then there were muffled voices. The Wraith inched closer to the conversation until only five yards separated them.

The voices were clear now, and the conversation was somewhat animated.

"Dad, can we trust those people across the river?"

"Son, I don't know, but I had a good feeling about that Bob Karr. He pitched in and saved those people on the crashed plane."

"But we don't know him. His people could rob us, and then we'd be fighting Karr's people, O'Berg and the Sheriff. That O'Berg will try to take over this entire area."

"I think you are right about that bastard. How he keeps his seat in the senate is beyond me."

"Bribes, blackmail, and crooked deals. That's how."

"I wish he'd have stayed in Washington. The sheriff doesn't have the brains God gave a goose. We could handle that slimy bastard, but both of them will be a handful."

Suddenly several lights came on, and they heard, "Hands up. This is the police. Drop those rifles."

"You're on private property."

"Screw your private property. You were committing treason by planning to kill the Senator and the sheriff. I have orders to shoot on sight anyone trying to overthrow our government. Kneel down and prepare to meet God or the devil."

Two Deputies tied Jim Dickerson's and his son's hands behind their backs.

The other Deputy drew his revolver and said, "Do you have anything to say or perhaps say a prayer before you receive your punishment."

Jim said, "Screw you, the Sheriff, and that crooked O'Berg."

"Well, that wasn't n...."

There was a soft noise off to the side, and a hole appeared in the Deputy's head; the other two were slow to react, and another hole appeared in a second Deputy's head followed by two holes in the thirds Deputy's chest. The first two fell immediately, but the third stood there for a few seconds until there was another pfift sound from the bushes and a bloody hole was made in his head. He fell at Jim's feet.

"I've got a gun on you so don't turn around," a muffled voice behind them said as their bindings were cut.

The Wraith poked a piece of paper in both men's pocket and said, "The note says, "The Wraith killed these men." Throw the bodies in the river, run their vehicle into the river, and forget this happened. Don't turn around."

Jim replied, "But you saved our lives, and we want to thank you."

All he heard was silence, so he turned around, and no one was there.

They tied bags full of rocks to the bodies, shoved them in the river, and then pushed the old car in with them.

The dark clad figure resembled a Wraith as it darted into the bushes when the patrol vehicle passed by along the fence. Since the lights went out the country was very dark unless there was a full moon. The moon wasn't full and hid behind a cloudy sky, which made it easy for the shadowy figure to move around the area undetected. The Wraith had made this trip several times. Taking out the trash was only a part time hobby for this vigilante.

Rumor had it there was a small biker gang that had set up their headquarters northwest of Carthage at the abandoned racetrack. Several young girls had disappeared since they arrived and two men were killed when they refused to give their food to the gang. These men were a blight on society, and the gang would continue to grow in size until they took over the entire area.

The Wraith hadn't been this far from home base before; however, the vermin had been dealt with within three miles of the Wraith's home base. The old car had been stashed yesterday for just this reason, to extend the reach of the person dressed in black with the camo face paint, compound bow and silenced .22 Ruger MKIII.

The old Pinto was traveling at 25 MPH with its lights off and barely made a sound. It had recently been painted primer black and could not be seen in the dark. It was 1:30 am, no one was out, and only a few dogs barked to split the eerie silence of the night. There was a slight wisp of fog lying close to the ground, and it was getting thicker as the Wraith got closer to the target.

The Wraith parked the car in a thicket just northwest of Highway 80 and Highway 25 junction. The Wraith stayed in the dark by walking in the tree line along the river. It was a short walk just a Driver and a # 6 Hybrid to the first building. The Wraith missed golf about as much as anything else since the lights went out.

There were two guards posted. One was up by the entrance and the other on the south end of the complex. The one up by the road rested in the ditch bleeding out from a gash on his

199

throat. The other guard was fast asleep or drunk, but the Wraith didn't care because he would soon join the other one in Hell. The Wraith had recently introduced over a dozen of the worst scum the world has to the Devil. Thanks to this effort, the area around Dixon Springs and the Horse Shoe were much more secure for the hard working survivors.

The man was snoring loudly, his shotgun hung from his neck by a piece of paracord, and he stank of beer. The Wraith slid the shotgun around behind him and twisted the gun around until the cord cut into the man's neck. He woke to find himself choking to death. He waved both arms and twisted to find the person strangling him. In a final desperate lunge, he grabbed the Wraith's shirt, and flipped the body over his head and slammed the Wraith to the ground.

Just as he thought he would be able to untangle the paracord from around his neck, the Wraith beckoned him to lean over to the dark figure. He did. The Wraiths free hand thrust upward to jab a knife into the man's eye piercing his brain. His agony was over, but the Wraith still had work to do.

The Wraith popped the left shoulder back in place by pushing against the building's wall and went about the business of removing trash from the Earth.

The first building only had supplies and water stored. The next one held over twenty women and their kids. All were slaves owned by the biker gang and were used and abused by the gang members. Most were being stockpiled for trade later to other evil like-minded people.

The Wraith allowed these people to sleep and moved on to the last building, which was the new home of the gang. The inside of the building held the concession stands and offices for the racetrack. Each office held one of the higher ranking officers of the gang and his current woman. The Wraith chose the nicest office first and slipped into the office without a sound. There were two young girls in the bed but were chained to the footboard of the bed. The man in the bed was naked and smelled like piss and stale beer. The Wraith placed one razor sharp knife on the man's throat and another against his genitals.

For an instant, their eyes locked, and the Wraith said, "Die you son of a bitch."

Then the dark figure cut his throat and neutered him at the same time. He died knowing his manhood had been sliced from his body.

The Wraith was lucky, as thug after thug was offered up to God or the Devil. The Wraith thought that if a mistake were made, God would sort it out in the afterlife. Only one teen girl woke up to see the Wraith slit her rapist's throat, and she thanked the Wraith. The Wraith fished a set of keys out of the man's pants pocket, unlocked the girl's chains, gave her the keys, and told her to unlock the others after the Wraith left.

The girl replied, "But the men will kill me."

"Darling, they will all be in Hell when I leave. Tell everyone the Wraith killed these men and freed you."

Six offices now held six dead gang bangers, and there were 12 more that needed to die. The Wraith had the guard's shotgun in one hand and the silenced Ruger in the other. The pistol made a popping sound ten times before the Wraith changed magazines to shoot the remaining two criminals. Drunks were easy to shoot as they lay passed out.

The dark clad figure chose a long white wall on the outside of the building and wrote THE WRAITH KILLED THESE CRIMINALS in capital letters with a can of black spray paint.

The Wraith then told the girl to help the others escape and suggested they head over to Carthage. The girl asked for the Wraith's name and if she could see the Wraith's face, but the Wraith just turned and left.

The Wraith had to avoid people walking on the road for the first time in her numerous excursions. Many of them were families heading south out of the larger Kentucky cities. They were tired, hungry, and desperate. They would be killing for food in a day or two. Several tried to stop her, but the Wraith avoided them by running off the road. The Wraith made it back to the car's hiding spot, and the Wraith crept back to the home base without being detected or missed for that matter.

It had been a busy night and a long one for the Wraith. Two attacks on opposite sides of the Horseshoe and dozens of criminals taken out of play. The Wraith was exhausted but very happy.

Bob woke up when the bed rocked and said, "Jane are you okay? It's almost daylight. Can't you sleep?"

"Sorry, I was having trouble sleeping and went to the outhouse. The stars are beautiful outside, and I had to stop and gaze at them for a while. Men always fall asleep after sex. It made me wide awake."

"Come on back to bed, and we can have an encore."

Jane was exhausted later that morning as she and Bob came out of his room and walked to the kitchen together. Will saw them try to sneak out of Bob's room, waved at his Grandparents, and gave them thumbs up. Maddie caught the wave, saw them, and gave thumbs up sign.

Jane walked into the kitchen and said, "I want you to meet my family. Family this is my new boyfriend, Bob. We have moved in together and don't need any harassment from any of you."

Jo exclaimed, "I knew this would happen if we didn't supervise you two. Mom, are you pregnant?"

Maddie and Will began laughing, and Will said, "Papaw don't knock her up."

"Screw you."

"Okay, cut it out. Bob has had the hots for me for years. I finally succumbed to his charm. We don't plan on having any children but could change our minds."

Jane said, "Jake go fetch a couple of bottles of water from the back porch. Mom, now that Jake is gone, you two need to move to the room at the far end of the house. We couldn't sleep for all of the unholy noise going on for hours."

Bob gave her the finger and said, "Too bad there's no noise coming from your room."

Missy replied, "You know Will, Maddie, and I are in the room."

Bob laughed and said, "Jane my dear, it might be time for us to move another trailer into the yard. The kids are grown and need a place of their own.

Izzy waved for Bob to come over to the gate and said, "That was Ralph from over toward Carthage. He lives close to the Race Track. He told me that someone killed a whole biker gang that was terrorizing the area. Said most were killed in their sleep. He also said that there are reports that a dozen other outlaws have been killed this week. The only common thing tying the killings together is that they are on the other side of the river from the Horseshoe. Criminals are being killed all around us."

"Well, that's good news. Isn't it."

"Yes, but everyone thinks we are doing the killing, and a couple of gangs have threatened to wipe us out."

"That's not good. We don't want attention drawn to this place."

Greg walked into the conversation and said, "It's impossible for us to stay below the radar. Bob, there are three dump trucks, two backhoes and two bulldozers working from dawn to dusk building our wall. Hell, just pounding the steel beams into the ground can be heard for miles.

There isn't any noise to hide our operation since the lights went out. No highway noise, no radios, iPods, or anything else. Hell one of our guards told me last night that several groups have spies watching us from the other side of the river. These are just curious people, but they talk to others, and soon everyone knows what we're doing."

"It's worse than I thought; I was a fool to think we could stay below the radar. People are beginning to starve, and many of the walkers are getting more adamant that we have food and we have to share it with them. We're going to end up with a massacre at the front gate if they try to rush us.

Those damn city people even think they can eat the corn they see planted closer to town. They trampled Jones' farm trying to find ears of corn on ten-inch tall stalks. I'm doubling the guard, and we'll build some tall guard towers and plate them with steel. If we can't avoid being noticed, we'll go the other way and scare the hell out of these desperate people. Perhaps they'll see our fortifications and go on down south to easier pickings.

Damn, we are ahead of any possible timeline for surviving this apocalypse, but the outlaws and thugs are just a step behind us. All the fiction I read on the Apocalypse says that it takes weeks for the thugs to run rampant."

Greg answered, "My guess is that most wardens at prisons let their prisoners loose on the world instead of letting them slowly starve to death. Most were already part of gangs and gangs are organized. With the government, military and local law enforcement falling apart there is no one to confront the bastards."

Bob and Jack checked on the progress on the wall that morning at lunchtime and saw Will and Maddie eating lunch in the shade of a tree.

Bob, I think that girl will make a fine wife for Will. She is a hard worker and knows how to handle herself in a scrap. Hell, she's probably the best long distance shooter that we have in our group."

"I really like her too. She is funny and very smart besides being beautiful. Will told me that she only wants him as a friend and she wants an older man. Will is a very smart and strong man. I hope Maddie realizes that before too long."

"Hell, a hundred years ago people would think Will is a grown man, and Maddie is an old maid at seventeen. Parents would be begging their son to find a decent young lady and settle down after he was 15 or so."

"I'm afraid that we are backing up 150 years in society and technology. Unfortunately, medical science is heading backward also. People will die from a rotten tooth or even a minor wound."

They saw Jane drive up and Bob said, "I should have told you, Jane and I have moved in together. I guess we'll get married soon."

"Hello, Jack did Bob tell you that we've moved in together? I hope to make him an honest man one day."

"Congratulations."

"Hey, while I have you two together, I'd like to take a scavenging party across the river and hit some of the abandoned shops across the river from Carthage. We need some women's and girl's clothes, hygiene products and lots of toilet paper. I'll take Maddie, Will and a couple of the men for security. We'll row across, gather as much as possible, and get back home quickly.

We'll naturally look for other items on our list, but focus on the target items."

"Sounds good. When do you plan to go?"

"I'd like to be at the strip mall at sun up. Most people are sleeping in these days except our little community. I'd like to get there, find the stuff, and be back before too many people are up and stirring around. We'll take a radio along and adjust the plan as needed."

"Okay, I'll get two volunteers and have them at Bob's house at 4:00 am."

Bob replied, "I'll be one of the volunteers."

Jane stopped to let Will know that the scavenging trip was on for in the morning and then headed over to the guard shack to help instruct the new guards.

*

Chapter 14

Day Seven – We're From the Government...

Coyotes howling woke Maddie up a little after midnight scaring her, so she tiptoed down to Will's room. Will was sound asleep when she lifted the covers and slid into bed with him. He was lying on his back without a shirt on; she gently laid her head on Will's bare chest and fell asleep secure in his arms.

Will woke up about 2:00 am and was pleasantly surprised that Maddie was in his arms with her head on his chest. He could feel her warm breath on his chest and hugged her tight. He rubbed her back with his right hand under her t-shirt and knew this was the one for him. He knew that he had to keep her safe at all cost and that making her happy was his major goal in life. He prayed that she would eventually feel the same way about him. He continued rubbing her back after he felt her waking up.

"Damn you feel good against me. Keep rubbing my back; it feels so good."

"Maddie, I love you, and you just want me for a friend. Then you crawl into bed with me. You are driving me crazy.

"Will the Coyotes scared me. I feel so safe in your arms, and you feel so good. I'm sorry I'm sending mixed messages. Please don't stop being my friend."

"Maddie it gets hard being your friend. I don't know if I should make love to you or shake your hand. I'll always be your friend, but after tonight, please don't get in bed with me again. It hurts too much that you don't care about me the way I care about you."

She didn't answer, and they fell asleep in each other's arms and slept until there was a soft knock on the door. No one answered, and Jane walked into the trailer. She saw them curled up together in bed and shook Will's shoulder.

"Son, wake up it's time to leave."

Will woke up; saw his Grandma looking down at him and Maddie. He started to talk, but Jane said, "Later and don't worry, I won't tell," and patted him on the shoulder."

Will woke Maddie up and said, "Maddie we're late. We need to dress and go!"

She hugged him and went back to her room to dress.

As they walked to the house, Will told Maddie, "Grandma caught us in bed this morning when she came over to see why we were running late. She told me that she wouldn't tell on us. I'll talk with her and explain that we didn't do anything."

"Are you trying to protect my honor?"

"Yes, but I also don't want to lose the trust of my parents. They trusted us to sleep in the same trailer without hooking up."

"We only lay there."

"I know, and I know you aren't interested in me, but will they believe me? Hell, I don't believe me. You felt so good last night it took all my willpower not to try something."

"That's because you care for me and are an honorable man."

"Then why am I so frustrated and pissed off? Maddie, I promise you that you won't ever find a man who loves you more than I do or who will take care of you as good as I will."

Will pulled her close, kissed her, and walked into the kitchen.

"Will," she called, but he kept walking away.

They rowed as quietly as possible and didn't talk as they crossed the river. Their first goal was to check out the Bait and Tackle Store and the small adjoining gas station and market just across the river. They weren't expecting much; however, the next shop, a clothing consignment shop, was two miles west. After that, there was a small strip mall about five miles from their boat landing.

They brought two collapsible shopping carts with them that had large wheels that helped the carts roll easily across grass or on the road.

They landed the two boats, hid them in the grass with two men guarding them, and then walked up the bank toward the road. The stores were only a tenth of a mile away so it only took a few minutes to get to a point where they could check out the stores and see if there were any dangers.

Both stores were deserted and had been looted. The only useable items in the tackle store were lures, fishing line and lots of sinkers and bobbers. The market did have several racks of t-shirts, flip flops, and sunglasses. There also was an assortment of motor oil, antifreeze, and a host of auto related items.

Jane went into the women's restroom and came back with a bag full of tampons from the dispenser. She was smiling as though she'd found gold. Will broke the door down to the janitor's closet and found a goldmine of toilet paper, hand towels, soap, and detergent. They loaded the carts and took their booty back to the boats, where they loaded the boats up to make the trip to the other side.

"Carl, we're going to walk the two miles to the consignment store, load up the carts, and be back here in three hours at the most. If we're not back by then send out a search party," Bob said.

The walk to the consignment store was uneventful, and no one was out on the street. There was smoke coming from a couple of chimneys, and Will thought he caught a faint whiff of bacon frying as they arrived at the store.

"Will help us make sure no one is in the store then you can stand guard at the front of the store and Bob can watch the back side."

Many of the racks had been turned over, but the store was full of clothing for men, women, and kids. There were also numerous racks full of shoes. There wasn't anyone in the store so Will and Bob stood their posts while the ladies filled the carts.

"Maddie come here. Look what I found," cried Jane as she ran her hands through the piles of costume jewelry.

"There are several fake diamond rings and gold wedding bands. I'm taking some back to the house for Bob's and my wedding. We may never find real ones until the big die off as Bob calls it."

Maddie started looking at the jewelry and pocketed several nice looking rings for herself.

"Dear, when is the wedding?"

"What wedding? We are just friends. Will wants more, but I'm not ready for a boyfriend."

"Was that just a friend this morning? Wait, don't get mad. You were sleeping with your legs intertwined and Will's face on your boobs. That looked more like lovers than friends."

"I got scared and jumped into bed with him. He was asleep when I got in bed with him. I feel secure when I'm with Will. We really didn't do anything. He wants me, but I just don't know."

"Girl I know my Grandson, and he fell for you the first day. Were y'all careful last night?"

"Jane, I swear we didn't do anything other than lay together. He was asleep when I got under the covers with him. He didn't try anything at all."

"The boy is in love with you, and you don't care for him."

"I care for him, but not romantically. Jane, I want to be with him like a best friend, not a husband."

"Call me Mom. You need a Mom now, and I'm up to the task. My advice is to make up your mind very quickly. Will will soon move on and date one of those other pretty girls in our community and won't have time for you. Shit, his new girlfriend won't want him being around a beautiful woman like you."

The back door opened and they saw Bob walk in with his hands in the air, and three men wearing black Battle Dress Uniforms armed with M4s walked behind him.

"Drop your guns or your husband dies first."

Bob said, "Please drop your guns there are many more of them outside."

Maddie and Jane lowered their weapons to the ground and raised their hands.

211

"Call the other man in, or I'll have a sniper pick him off."

Jane replied, "Hon go to the door and ask your husband to come on in."

Maddie went to the front door and called, "Will come on in; we need some help."

Will entered the room, and two men grabbed him from the side while the other kept their rifles trained on the others.

Bob keyed the mic on the walkie-talkie in his pants and said, "Who are you and why are you bothering us?"

"We are with FEMA, and you are looters. You're lucky we didn't shoot you."

"Hey, we're just trying to survive. We were caught down here visiting relatives and didn't have any clothes. This store is abandoned and had already been looted."

"So stealing is stealing get your asses moving you have a long ride ahead to the FEMA camp in Cherokee. Men in the truck on the right and women in the left one."

"Sarge they are married. They go on the bus."

"Damned Army is getting soft and won't separate families."

They stepped up into the bus to see the bus was half-full of couples and a few children. There were two guards at the front of the bus, who took turns watching the detainees and talking with the driver.

Bob walked to the back of the bus to get as far away from the guards as possible. As he passed one couple, he keyed the mic and asked, "Where are the FEMA people taking us?"

"Some place in Alabama called Cherokee. There is a big FEMA camp there, and they take looters to the prison and honest people to the camp."

212

"With everyone mixed together how can they tell who is a looter and who isn't?"

"We were walking down the road, and they stopped us and told us we were looters."

"I thought as much," Bob said as he took his hand off the walkie-talkie."

"Jack, someone captured our team across the river. I could hear Bob talking on the walkie-talkie with a couple of different people. The first was a soldier working for FEMA. He called our team looters. They are heading to a FEMA camp located in Cherokee Alabama."

"Greg, let's call a council meeting."

The group took an hour to get to Greg's house. The meeting began with Greg filling them in on everything he heard.

Jo demanded that they take action, "We have to go get them and set them free. That's half of our family."

Jack replied, "I'll lead a team over to the other side to find out what happened and if there are any witnesses. Then we'll decide if we are going to go after them."

"Bill and I will go with you across the river, and I'm telling you right now that we are going after them even if it's just Bill and me."

"Calm down Jo."

"I am calm. You don't want to fucking see me when I'm mad."

The bus had been on the road for an hour when Jane leaned over and whispered to Bob, "How did you hide the walkie-talkie? The bastards searched us."

"Just pure old luck. It was tucked in the front of my pants and fell down my pants when they searched me. He didn't spend any time feeling my junk."

"The SOB felt mine for way too long."

"Point the bastard out, and I'll kill him when I get a chance."

"I'll take care of him in my own time and way."

"That doesn't surprise me at all."

Will interrupted and asked, "Are we going to try to escape before we get to the camp?"

"Son, I'm watching for a chance. We may have to wait until we stop. Overpowering three guards on this bus in motion with us being in the middle of a convoy doesn't look too promising. These Blackman Mercenaries do the dirty work for the government. They will shoot and ask questions later.

They didn't get a chance to escape even though they stopped three times during the six-hour trip to the camp. When they made rest stops, the guards sent the men to one side of the bus and the women on the other.

"Ladies, my men won't be watching you do your business in the bushes; however, I will personally shoot any man whose wife doesn't get back on the bus. Ladies if you want to run away be my guest. It will be a clean divorce."

No one ran away during the three stops. The guards handed out a bottle of water and an MRE to each captive at the second stop. The guard passing out the meals said, "We only get paid for the live ones that we get to the prison. We don't want you

214

to die of starvation or tell the Army that we mistreated you bunch of crooks."

The convoy wound its way through Lebanon, Nashville, Springhill, and Columbia Tennessee on its way to the Alabama state line. The cities were a maze of stalled and wrecked cars with hundreds of fires still burning almost a week after TSHTF. The convoy dodged cars as it made its way south, never getting over 30 MPH. The speed picked up a bit when they turned onto Highway 43 South at Columbia. The road only had a few cars per mile.

Florence, Alabama was a smoking wreck. Bob waved for one of the guards and asked what happened to Florence.

"When the power went out the guards at the local prison all left to go home. The warden didn't want the prisoners to starve in their cells, so he started releasing the non-violent offenders. Some of them overpowered the warden and the few remaining guards and set all of the prisoners free. They tortured and killed the guards and warden and then took over Florence and went on a murder and rape spree. They killed thousands and set the city on fire in a drunken rage.

We sent in two companies and killed every one of the drunken murderers. We lost 120 men in that fight. That's why we can't stand you criminals and looters."

The convoy rolled up to a large fence that had razor ribbon piled on both sides and stopped to be searched before entering. Each vehicle was cleared and sent to the staging area in front of several large tents. There were several dozen armed men and five machine gun emplacements around the captives as they unloaded from the bus.

The leader of the Blackman troops called everyone to attention and said, "You are now leaving the custody of the Blackman Company and into the capable hands of the US Army who along with FEMA operate this detention facility. Men will advance toward the Sergeant and go into the door to his left and women will go into the door on his right.

You will strip down and receive a delousing shower, new clothes, a pillow, a blanket, and a bunk assignment. You will then rejoin your spouse, go to your assigned bunk and await further instructions. It would behoove you to start lining up so that you enter the door with your spouse so we don't have lost people. MOVE!"

A large man with a clipboard dressed in Army fatigues and Staff Sergeant's stripes took a count as the captives passed him. He was singing, "You're in the Army now."

Will and Bob kept watching the women's line and adjusted their position to match the girls so they wouldn't be separated any longer than necessary. The line barely stopped long enough for them to strip off their clothes and shoes. They walked from the undressing room straight into a shower room where they were handed a pair of goggles and men were hosing them down with a foul smelling concoction as they continued to walk. The stuff was under high pressure, so the men cupped their hands over their privates as they were blasted by the liquid.

Next, they walked into a regular shower room where the showers rinsed the smelly disinfectant from their bodies. They were given a towel and told to quickly dry off and move on to the clothing line where they were issued a pair of underwear, t-shirt, pants and flip-flops.

They quickly dressed and moved to the next line where they received a pillow, two sheets, a blanket, and were given a plastic tag with a bunk number. Bob and Will walked out into the massive tent and saw the numbers on the ends of the bunk beds.

"Well, we just wait for our women and get our bunks. Damn, these are the old regulation single bunk beds."

A guard heard him and replied, "Yes and I hope you like your old lady because you both have to share the one mattress. We believe in efficiency. Oh, and if you get frisky on the bottom bunk, you will make the people above you sea sick."

"Will, here I am," shouted Maddie as she ran toward him with Jane right behind her.

"That was one of the worst experiences of my life," Jane told them as she hugged Bob, then added, "Those women were sadists. That spray stripped my skin off."

Bob couldn't help but laugh as he said, "Did you two lose something?"

Maddie turned red and said, "The bitches took our bras and didn't have any to replace them with. They also gave us men's briefs. No sexy underwear in this place."

Bob smiled and replied, "Sometimes less is more."

Bob took Jane's arm and started down Row T to find bunk 17A. They walked for several yards and found the bunk. Will's was a few feet away and was S17A. Bob said ladies this is our home for a while.

Jane said, "Damn, one of us has to sleep on the top bunk. That's no fun."

"Jane and Maddie, that's not how it works. You sleep with your hubby on the bottom bunk. Another couple has the top bunk."

Jane replied, "Well, that's not too bad. We..."

It then dawned on her that her Grandson would be sleeping every night with Maddie. She thought *how soon are you and Will planning on getting married?*

Will replied, "Grandma, it's not like we could do anything with a couple four feet above us and you and Papaw three feet over there."

"I'll overlook that stupid remark since you are an inexperienced young man. Son where there's a will there's a way when it comes to young girls and boys with hormones raging," said Jane.

"I'll bet that includes Grandparents also."

"Watch it, boy. Hey, shut up. People are heading this way."

The bottom bunks all around them filled up quickly, and then the top bunks began to fill up. A young couple walked up to Bob's bunk, and the man said, "Crap, we have a top bunk. People could die from the fall. Anyone want a top bunk?"

There was a round of hell no's."

"Hey, this is my wife Doris, and I'm AJ Norman. How are y'all doing besides the obvious?"

Will and Bob introduced themselves and their spouses to the young couple.

Bob asked, "Where are you two from?"

"We're from Arkansas. We were on vacation and headed to Florida when the event happened. We made it back this way from Mobile and were picked up in Helana, Arkansas on the Mississippi River. We only had to make it 50 more miles, and we would have been home free. My dad has a big farm there, and I know we would have had plenty of food."

"Why did they capture you?"

"They said we were looting because we were searching cars to find food."

"Pretty much the same here except we were at my home in Tennessee. Good ta' meet ya' anyway."

Then a voice came over the loudspeakers and said, "Row Z walk to the front of your row, turn right and go out the door to the mess hall. A soldier will help direct you this time. Now Row Y tag on to row Z. You get the picture follow the row in front of you until I stop the line when the mess hall is full. Next meal starts with Row Y."

They called row S, and Bob and Jane joined Will and Maddie in line. Twenty minutes later, they had their hot meal and seated at one of the rows of picnic tables in a large row of large tents with picnic tables.

The meal consisted of a small bowl of oatmeal, corn, and something that looked and tasted like a slice of Spam. They also received a glass to fill with water.

"Not half bad if you like mush and Spam," said Bob.

"I wonder what we will do for recreation and something to fight boredom."

"If it's like the Army, they'll keep us busy even if it's stacking and restacking the same bricks. We need to watch every move the guards make and figure out their schedules, commit to memory the layout of the camp so we can make a map to help us later," Bob said as he changed topics as other people sat down beside them.

They got wet walking back to their bunks since it started raining while they finished their supper. The rain brought in a cold front, and their tent was chilly.

They quickly found out where the bathrooms were and another announcement said, "Be in your bunks five minutes after we announce lights out and stay there until lights on at 5:00 am. Now since there are only a few lights that the guards use we don't actually turn any lights off and on. Just do what you're told and you won't get shot trying to go outside.

Now I know you've been asking why there are two 5-gallon buckets with a roll of TP in each one by your bunks. Now you know what to do if you need to go in the middle of the night."

Maddie said, "Oh shit."

"Please no shit. There aren't any tops on those buckets," replied Jane.

Maddie replied, "I don't want to squat on a bucket in front of 200 people either."

"I guess we can take turns holding up our blankets if someone has to go in the night."

The speaker came back on, and the announcer added, "I know many of you are new to our little luxury hotel here in Cherokee. Yes, there are two people to a bunk. I don't care what you do, but if you fight or start a fight, you will be moved to a bunk outside in the rain. Sleep tight."

Will stripped down to his underwear; however, Maddie kept her t-shirt and pants on as they went to bed. They crawled into the narrow bed and lay face to face so they could talk in a low whisper. The people above them went to bed earlier.

They lay on their sides and tried to talk in a low whisper.

"Will I'm so scared. We don't know what these men will do to us."

"Don't worry, I'll protect you. Maddie, I will die before one of them hurts you."

Maddie snuggled up to Will and said, Will, wrap your legs around mine. I'm scared and freezing, and you are so warm."

Will took his t-shirt off and helped Maddie put it on over top of hers and then wrapped his arms around her and placed his leg on top of hers to share their body warmth.

"Maddie, I'm sorry that you have to go through this. I'll do my best to get you back home as soon as possible."

She said, "You are my hero."

Will held her tight and replied, "Maddie, I'll always be there for you."

They stopped talking and listened to the sounds around them. Two bunks to the left a woman was crying. The bunk above Bob and Jane was moving too much but stopped moving after a while. Will had to cover Maddie's mouth with his hand to keep her from laughing aloud.

"Shush, go to sleep girl, or I'm going to pinch you."

"I'll pinch back, and we'll be thrown out in the rain."

Maddie rolled over and pulled Will's arm over the top of her. They lay there spooned together all night.

Will fell asleep more in love with Maddie than ever before and knew he must win her over.

The trip across the river didn't yield much. They found the carts in the consignment shop and no signs of their family. Jo saw a woman on a porch across from the consignment shop and went over to question her.

"Hello, did you see any vehicles here this morning?"

"Why yes, there were some military people come through in a convoy. They arrested some looters and drove off."

That night had a terrible turn of events for the people at the Horseshoe. A large group of the near do wells from the Dixon Springs area decided to take their fair share of what the people in the Horseshoe had gathered. They were poorly armed but had shotguns and deer rifles.

Since the fence and wall had been completed, their only means to make an attack and take what they thought belonged to them was to take boats across the river, kill anyone who resisted and to take the food and weapons back by boat. The idiots thought that drinking their last bottles of booze was a good idea before attacking the Horseshoe, so many of them were drunk as they manned their boats.

The alcohol wasn't conducive to keeping silent as they fumbled their way across the river. Jack's son Tony was the first to hear them, and he radioed Jack and Greg to spread the alarm. Thanks to the noise, Jack had all of his fighters waiting on the gang who couldn't row straight or be silent.

Jack waited until they were pulling the boats onto shore and began shooting. The drunks began firing their guns randomly at anything that moved until they ran out of bullets. The clowns were caught in a crossfire and massacred before most of them stepped onto the shore. Jack kept his people shooting as long as there was movement. Every one of the attackers was killed that night.

Unfortunately several of the team were hit by stray bullets and lucky shots made by the attackers. Bill received a load of number 7 shot from a 12 Gauge in the back. Lucky for him the shot came from a hundred feet away, and only seven pellets hit him, and his coat slowed them down. Tony was hit by a .30 .30 in the calf and Betty Lou caught a ricochet in the left upper arm.

Jo helped pick out the buckshot from Bill after he took care of Tony and Betty Lou. He hurt like hell, but the wounds weren't serious. Jo used fine point tweezers to pluck out the pellets and poured alcohol on the wounds to keep them from becoming infected. She then applied an antiseptic salve and placed Band-Aids on his back.

"Jo, we're still tending to Missy's wound, and now my back will keep me close to home for a while. I don't see how we can go looking for our family."

"Bill, you are right. We can't go, but I can and will go get my mom, son, and Bob. I'm a cop. That's what cops do. We chase down bad guys and find lost people. I'll try to get some volunteers, but I'm going to Cherokee and getting my family back."

"Jo, take Max, he will help protect you."

THE END

A complete list and description of all of my books follow.

If you like my novel, please post a review on Amazon.

To contact the Author, please leave comments @:

www.facebook.com/newmananthonyj   Facebook page.

To view other books by AJ Newman, go to Amazon to my Author's page:

A list and description of my other books start on the next page.

http://www.amazon.com/-/e/B00HT84V6U

Thanks,   A.J. Newman

*

Books by A J Newman

A Family's Apocalypse Series:
Cities on Fire
Family Survival (July 2017)

After the Solar Flare - a Post-Apocalyptic series:
Alone in the Apocalypse   Adventures in the Apocalypse*

After the EMP series:
The Day America Died New Beginnings
The Day America Died Old Enemies
The Day America Died Frozen Apocalypse

"The Adventures of John Harris" - a Post-Apocalyptic America series:
Surviving   Hell in the Homeland   Tyranny in the Homeland
Revenge in the Homeland...Apocalypse in the Homeland   John
Returns

"A Samantha Jones Murder Mystery Thriller series:
Where the Girls Are Buried   Who Killed the Girls?

Books by A J Newman and Cliff Deane

Terror in the USA: Virus: – Strain of Islam

These books are available at Amazon:

http://www.amazon.com/-/e/B00HT84V6U

Books by A J Newman and Cliff Deane

Virus: - Strain of Islam

Three years ago, CIA Agent Max Owens was captured and tortured by the Taliban because they thought he had information concerning a bioweapon the Saudis were developing to use against them. Several hundred villagers died and then nothing happened.

Now a biological attack on New York City leaves thousands dead and millions hospitalized in several countries. The USA is terrorized. No terrorist group claims the attack. Was this the major attack or a sample of things to come? Was this the end of the attacks or the first that leads to a worldwide apocalypse?

In this bioterrorism thriller, radical Islamic terrorists use genetic engineering to develop a deadly strain of virus based on the Ebola and Zika viruses. Their goal is to eradicate non-Muslims, bring forth the Twelfth Imam and begin the World Caliphate.

Can Max Owens and his team of CDC and CIA operatives find and stop this terrorist group before they unleash this Strain of Islam and kill billions of people?

http://www.amazon.com/-/e/B00HT84V6U

225

*

Also from AJ Newman

The Sun is entering a period of solar activity that makes the famous Carrington event of 1859 pale by comparison. Just that alone will knock out the grid, kill most vehicles and fry electronics. The USA is not prepared for this catastrophe, and the entire world will go back 150 years in technology and living standards. Hardened military vehicles and pre-electronic vehicles will be the only machines moving not drawn by a horse, mule or camel. People with pacemakers will fall dead, planes will fall out of the sky and transportation will come to a halt. People will starve; riots and looting will start all across the world. 60% of the world's population will die off the first year.

Alone in the Apocalypse is a post-apocalyptic tale about a series of solar events that test the mettle of a man who just wants to live alone in remote Wyoming. Will the solar catastrophe or his fellow man kill him, or can he prevail?

What would you do to survive? Read "Alone in the Apocalypse and find out what Matt Jones does to survive.

Adventure in the Apocalypse continues Matt's story. He has been stranded on a small sailboat with no memory and only his wits to survive. He feels that he has to find someone but can't remember whom they are or for that matter who he is. Mary and Patty have been separated from him, and they have to make it on their own in a hostile world with danger lurking around every corner. Attacks by pirates are offset by meeting new friends as the saga continues. Will Matt get his memory back? Which lady is his soul mate and will he ever see her again? Those are the questions, and this last book in the series will answer those questions.

Also from AJ Newman

After The EMP

The Day America Died New Beginnings - Zack Johnson is stranded on the west coast when an EMP attack destroys the Grid. He must get home to find and protect his daughter. This is a tale about what he has to do to get home and survive. It's also a story about the people he meets along the journey. Many are great people, but some are thugs that have to be dealt with.

The Day America Died Old Enemies continues the story with Zack and his family encountering disease, attacks from enemies and friends and a dictator trying to take over the community that has been his home. Zack's team also comes up with some hacks that improve life and put them on the way back to a more modern lifestyle.

The Day America Died Frozen Apocalypse has Zack and team starting over after being driven from their homes to a hideout in the woods near their hometown. The USA was attacked with nuclear EMP weapons has no power and food is in short supply. The government has not helped, and there is a power struggle between the forces of good and evil. It is now mid winter, and while Zack and his friends prepared for survival, many of their neighbors are cold and starving. The new mayor has taken control of the food supply and only doles it out to his supporters. What can Zack do?

http://www.amazon.com/-/e/B00HT84V6U

The Adventures of John Harris:

This series of six Post-Apocalyptic novels tells how John Harris leads a group of survivors through the chaos of a country that has fallen apart. Rogue US Government officials and a coalition of Third World Leaders have launched a major nuclear and EMP attack on all of the major powers and killed over 100 million Americans. The grid is down, and water and food are scarce. The USA is in chaos with criminals and thugs attacking innocent citizens while the DHS is placing millions in relocation camps. John and his team fight back!

http://www.amazon.com/-/e/B00HT84V6U

Also from AJ Newman

A Samantha Jones Murder Mystery Thriller

A teenage girl solves a series of kidnappings and murders of young girls. The teen girl is stalked by her mom's boyfriend and almost killed by a high-ranking political figure. How are the two crimes linked? This unlikely crime fighter solves the puzzle of **"Where the Girls Are Buried."**

In the next novel in the series, she solves **"Who killed the Girls?"** Was it the high ranking politician or was it his son? Who is behind the attacks on their families? Why don't they want these crimes solved?

http://www.amazon.com/-/e/B00HT84V6U

About the Author

A J Newman is the author of over a dozen novels that have been published on Amazon. He was born and raised in a small town in the western part of Kentucky. His Dad taught him how to handle guns very early in life, and he and his best friend Mike spent summers shooting .22 rifles and fishing.

He read every book he could get his hands on and fell in love with science fiction. He graduated from USI with a degree in Chemistry and made a career working in manufacturing and logistics, but always fancied himself as an author.

He served six years in the Army National Guard in an armored unit and spent six years performing every function on M48 and M60 army tanks. This gave him a great respect for our veterans who lay their lives on the line to protect our country and freedoms.

He currently resides in Kentucky with his wife Patsy and their three tiny mop dogs, Sammy Cotton, Callie and Benny.

Made in the USA
Middletown, DE
22 June 2017